I0519513

Patches of a Second-Hand Planet
Volume 1:
Where the Chill Meets the Sun

By Spun Counterguy

Interior Artwork by Huxley King and Spun Counterguy
Cover Artwork by Huxley King and Spun Counterguy
Cover and Interior Design by Terrence Boyce

An introduction and explanation:

I was walking through the paths that snake between hills and near-mountains when I heard some music, unmistakably being made on a flute that is made of roots. There weren't no one but me in the hills, so my mind slunk into thinking there were musical ghosts messing about.

But eventually my ear established the melodies were coming from a hole on the side of a particular mound. The hole was covered by crisscrossed roots, which gave the impression of a window — or bars, depending on your slant of light. The performance was nice and so I got comfortable next to the hole and listened for a good long spell.

Every day I came, and every day the musician deep down in the mound played. Eventually he became aware of my ears and we began to converse. He wouldn't say who put him in what come to find out was a prison but did say why, which was because of the stories he knew. Of course anything that would cause a power to wet its pants enough to imprison a guy over, we'd all want to know about. So I asked him to tell me the stories. And here they are.

My apologies for the abrupt change of art style that occurs about halfway through the book. The artist who sat with me outside the mound and sketched what the prisoner described, herself got imprisoned. Why or by whom I'm not sure but as soon as I get done writing this paragraph, I'm off to locate and liberate her. Thus some of the rudimentary drawings in the later chapters are my own. See I was nailed in the head by a broke-off chunk of the moon when I was 8 years old and so the art part of my brain was damaged. Thus my sketches (and some aspects of my maturity) will never progress past what you see here.

Ok — gotta go,
Spun Counterguy

Stories:

The Cold Man and the Old Face

There once was a man who was always so very cold.

So he went on a journey until he found a polite, nice woman in a nice polite land. And she kept him warm.

For a little while.

He got cold again and so they made a boy and a girl.

And they kept him warm.

For a little while.

The man got so terribly cold again that it drove him to a shivery madness. And he set his children and wife on fire.

This kept the man warm for a little while but because they all wept in terrible pain, the tears put out the fires.

The cold man became angry and accused them all of being selfish. At that, he set them on fire again. They all cried but he kept spraying them with gasoline and eventually the tears ran out.

The daughter jumped in a lake and swam away.

The wife ran off a short distance, used her blood to put out most of the fire but left a little bit burning so her husband could still see her and not try to re-light her.

The son decided to please his father and so let the flames consume his whole being and endured the flames as best as he could.

And this kept the man warm for a little while.

When the man became cold again, the son went hunting for people and brought them to his father already aflame. This kept the man warm but the son was sad because he liked many of the people he had lit up and brought to his father.

So the son suggested they build a pyre to keep super warm and they wouldn't have to burn any more people. When the now terrified people in the land heard of the son's idea, they gladly helped gather kindling and brush and other dead vegetation to fuel the cold man's fire.

And this kept the man warm. But of course only for a little while.

After which the man started throwing the helping people onto the pyre and they screamed in pain, many of them dying. This kept the man very warm but only while there was fresh people fuel on the pyre.

And so there was a great sadness and loss in the land, not to mention a drastic decline of the population and a terrible acrid smell. Which might've meant no more bodies to throw on the fire but nice unsuspecting people wander into terrible situations almost as often as terrified people flee from them. I mean who can turn down an invitation to become insatiably warm?

Now not terribly far away from all the fires lived what looked like a little girl with an old person's face. She wore what seemed like layers upon layers of cloths and loved to stand in the rain.

One day she happened to pass some crispy burnt people running and talking about the cold man and all his meanness.

The old face little girl was taken by the sad story and paid a neighbor to give her a ride on his pet sky mole. It only took a couple of burrowings out of a few clouds for her to spy the pyre and the flaming people, and to hear all the screaming.

Oldy Face decided to make a dirt puppet show about the cold man, to help warn people in the land not to come near him and to caution children not to grow up burning people. (reference note: If you've been through those parts, you already know this but if not, there are small trees called Root Reachers which for some often unfortunate reason directs it's roots down, over and then up. If you've tripped in the wilderness and looked back, saying to yourself, "Why were those roots reachin' for my ankles?" Well, then these are the roots we're talkin' bout.

Anyway, long ago someone thought to yank back at the exposed roots and discovered a tiny tree a short distance away whose branches moved this way and that. Eventually an arty-type person molded mud over the trees to look like people or animals and at a tug here and there at the roots, had dancing dirt bears or mouth-running dirt orators! Dirt puppet theaters became such a popular form of entertainment that naturally an organized mob of malcontents was formed to protest the practice, under the guise that covering the Root Reachers with mud was killing them and they had no choice in the matter. But the art world defended itself by pointing out that the trees were always in the middle of committing suicide when they were recruited into the theater life, the exposed, half-gnawed on and boot-scarred roots presented as evidence. But as most mobs who claim to speak for an unspeakable third party do, the protesters ignored the evidence and began disrupting performances, even killing a few dirt puppeteers by covering them in mud till they suffocated. Finally, Brother Nature threw it's hat in the ring and wiped out all the anti-dirt theater peoples by deeming their choice of nature-friendly vegetation-free diets as unsustainable and they all died of random deficiencies, common sense notwithstanding).

Yeah ok, back to the old faced little girl's dirt puppet shows, it was both a sad and funny work, showing all the suffering of the people and making the cold man look like a crazy wingnut. Sometimes past victims would attend the shows and laugh for the first time since they had been scorched. Other victims would run away mid-performance, screaming from the bad memories. And some of the past victims who stayed for the whole performance would leave crying out of pity for the man who hurt people to stay warm.

Although the dirt puppet show did help many people steer clear of the cold man, there was always somebody who got caught by the cold man's son. Oldy Face decided that the terror in their land was not going to completely stop until someone stopped the cold man from his hurtful deeds.

So she bravely ventured to the pyre and told the man he would never ever get contentedly warm setting everyone on fire. Strangely this is the first time the cold man had ever heard such criticism and he was stunned. (The people of this land were notoriously polite and were so proud of it, the graveyards were full of people who went there sooner than should have, never uttering a negative word.)

With a shaking rage, the appalled man returned, "I keep THEM warm when I burn them! They just can't see that I'm what doing to them is good for them!"

Here the old face little girl realized that the cold man had such a warped sense of reality that she'd probably have more luck asking a lipless rhinosepheres beast to close it's mouth when it ate baby crispy crunch birds.

And she said as much.

This insult infuriated the cold man and he threw much fire at Oldy Face! She shielded her face with her bundled arms and she remained unharmed.

This made the cold man livid and so his magnified his fire efforts by nuclear proportions! The old face little girl curled up in a ball and the mushroom blasts did not take root.

The cold man raged, stomped and screamed in a tantrum more powerful than ten thousand brats on a dead pony.

The son, eager to ease his father's pain, tackled the old face little girl, trying to set her a flame with his own fire. She did not burn but when he pulled at her limbs, he heard a ripping sound. The son soon discovered that the girl's body was just that of a rag doll's soaked with water.

He pulled and pulled until all the fabric was tore away and all that remained was a head and a heart, and those were now burning a little bit from the son's touch.

"What kind of soggy indescript creature are you?!!!" the cold man demanded.

"I'm just a person who's mother burnt most of me away when I was a little girl" she replied.

The son, who had been partially put out by all the soggy cloth, became empathetic with the old head and heart. So he used her torn wet body parts to dab out what flames he'd inflicted on her.

This betrayal incensed the cold man and he poured onto his son all the firepower and fuel he could muster. It was all too much and his son gave up living.

At seeing his dead son the cold man regretted his actions immediately and began to wail. His tears put out the remaining flames left on the old little girl, for which she thanked him for.

His fit ended at the girl's gratitude but still weeping he proclaimed to her, "Now that my son is dead, I'm colder than I've ever been! Can you help me get warm without hurting anyone?"

"You still have your daughter and wife" the head and heart offered.

He shook his cold head. "My wife keeps out of my reach and my daughter keeps out of my sight."

"A child who hasn't been burnt by one parent always stays close" the old head suggested. "I'm sure your wife knows where your daughter is."

So the cold man's eyes scanned the setting dark for his wife's contained fire. It was still for a time but then began to move.

He quietly followed his wife down to a lake, where she got into a boat and began to row out. He entered the water and swam noiselessly behind.

The boat settled on a small island, where the wife walked up into and up to a well. She spoke into the well, at which a voice the cold man recognized replied.

He approached the well crying in joy at hearing his daughter's voice again. His wife wiped his eyes with her burning hand and her pain finally ceased. The cold man's tears were overflowing and he took the well bucket to catch the liquid. He looked down in the well to his burnt little girl and offered the bucket. She accepted and he let down the rope, where she added the tears to her well water home.

And this made the cold man warm, somewhat.

The chill never did completely leave the cold man. With memories of those who still were in pain because of him (the author included), nameless peoples who were dead because of him, his son dead because of him, his daughter never leaving the safety of the well because of him, his wife left with a useless crunchy brittle arm and half-charred face because of him — it was all regrets so strong that it easily kept what warmth he'd acquired at bay.

But no one was on fire anymore, at least not by his hands (I'll not gonna lie to ya and say that peace completely returned the land. Some of his victims perpetuated the hurt put on them, becoming quite the deft fire starters, though minus some of the voracity).

And some people forgave the old man when he asked. Others accepted help from him when he offered, including the old face little girl, for whom he built a new woman's doll body with several exciting innovative features. (Side note: If you are ever in this land, ask folks about the "Old Face Hottie". You'll won't hear much about her dealings with the cold man, that legend forgotten, but you will hear about her heroic feats as a tank commander in the War Against The Puddlesniffers Of The East and how good she looked doing it!)

The old man died maybe a few years after he changed his low down ways. And when that happened, an incision was made into a high hill where no shade ever colored the ground. There, the old man was laid down into it and was finally warm without interruption.

Butterfly Lies

LidleLin spun off the Blinky Agespot Memorial Turnpike
on her Mutoe Chuh (a wooden device she'd built herself in
carpentry class, which both had practicability and cuteness
written all over it) and had to swerve a bit to avoid hitting
tourists posing for pictures with some roadside pitpan bears
that laid about every day at this spot, charging people for
photos with them. Pitpan bears were not indigenous to this
area so even though they couldn't be considered top-shelf
pitpans by any stretch of the imagination (they were unkept
and scruffy to say the least), the area folk didn't have much
of a reference point to compare them to. So at least a few
times a day, the opportunistic bears found a few suckas to
shell out a few bucks or cigarettes to get their photos taken
with them — the "dirty and unattractive pitpan bears", as
the town zoology students refereed to them.

The sight would usually bother LidleLin but today was a
big day in her little town of Winkyburg: it was the annual
Brain Cleaver Clever Competition! Abilities were
showcased during such show portions as Neuron Receptor
Pong, multitasking Debate (LidleLin planned on removing
a rotten tooth from a volunteer in the audience while
arguing the merits of free range Uh Oh Monster eggs),

Knock Knock Jokes With Meteor Owls and often some sort of artistic display of talent (LidleLin was ready to sing a selection from the musical, "Andy McDischarge Get Your Calculator, Sextant and Duct Tape".

I can tell you that after the competition was all said and done — not without some fierce competition from a local boy named Dunn Thunkit — LidleLin was declared the winner.

After the Puttin' The Clever Crown On-Ya-Head ceremony, the mother of another competitor — Snippy Plyers — praised the glowing LidleLin in front of everyone, stating, "LidleLin, I very much admire you and wish my child was as clever and sneaky as you. You must have great skill when greasing the judges' wheels." The woman was of course not praising LidleLin's brain cleaver clever ability but implying she'd won because she was good at cheating!

And as soon the mother said what she said, a butterfly made of words fluttered out of her mouth and flew up and into a nest that floated high above the village. This nest was where the town's collective memory and understanding were kept.

LidleLin stopped breathing at Snippy's mum's last letter of her sentence and in that butterfly saw all that she'd worked for honestly, fly away and settle into the nest of the Winkyburg citizen's minds. Not missing a beat, everyone in the town began praising LidleLin for her sneaky tip toe dishonesty, cheering and patting her on her cute little dishonest head.

In Mrs. Plyers' s defense, her admiration was just the collective common feeling in the town. In Winkyburg's then current culture, the ends always justified the means, even if it meant cheating, fudging, lying, finagling and making out with ugly people in power. Sadly the town was so notorious for corruption and glossy facades, that if a Winkyburg citizen ever traveled to other cities and said, "I graduated from Winkyburg University" the outsiders heard, "I might've really graduated from Winkyburg University but there's a good chance I actually just bribed my way all the way to the graduation ceremony, giving free kisses to cut in line to get my diploma even, and now I actually know so little — educationally speaking — that I can't even read that diploma. But I'll pay you to read it for me, if you're interested in making a few bucks...or gettin' some good lovin'." The outsider would then check their pockets and purses to make sure the Winkyburg citizen hadn't stolen their money already.

"Big butt backside drool!" the always honest LidleLin cursed and stomped later in her cute tiny legged ineffectual way in front of her best friend Shady. These two friends often — well only — met at this particular Castroni Nut Tree because as a small child Shady had been placed in the tree's crook by his mother and then had been forgotten (being a typical Winkyburg towns person, when the mother couldn't remember where she left her baby, she just stole someone else's). Shady told himself that something bad must've really happened to his mom because she also left a carton of her beloved Jaundiced Brand Cigarettes on one of the other branches that sad day (the mother also replaced the lost carton by cheating at a 'Guess Which Mental Illness This Woman With 203 Cats And Her Own Newsletter Has!' contest and winning the grand prize, which was a hay wagon full of the said cigarettes). The lonely child survived by eating the tree's puny nuts and insect dwellers. Over time the tree's bark skin grew over Shady's skin skin. He didn't have any friends at first (he couldn't really count the carton of cigarettes, also now absorbed into the tree) but eventually LidleLin bounced by and the two hit it off, she often bringing him water in the dry seasons and chasing away molasses poachers in the sappy seasons.

LidleLin felt he was the best kind of friend one could have in that he always had time for her and she always knew where to find him (unlike another one of LidleLin's friends Klorg Lintmouth, whom she complained once, "Klorg, not only are you ugly but you're difficult to locate").

"Why did Snippy's mom have to say those untrue things?" LidleLin continued, now kicking up in the air about where the mother's mouth would've been, had she been standing in front of LidleLin and Shady. "Now everyone thinks I'm clever in a crooked way and not clever in an straight way. All my studies and hard work are now questionable!"

Shady went to shrug but was interrupted by a creepy looking beady eyed man who saddled up to the girl and tree and posed to LidleLin, "Listen girl, do you think you could help my son pass his Nuclear Puffy Pockets class. He's never attended a lecture yet and the final exam is in an hour". (Also Shady was interrupted from shrugging by the fact that his shoulders were pinned down by the tree that had grown around his body many years ago.)

After LidleLin angrily jumped up in the air to perform an elbow punt to the beady eyed man's left eye, causing the father to run away to look for another way to save his son's academic career, Shady finally got a chance to answer LidleLin's question. "Mrs. Plyers probably said it because Snippy didn't win, so she had to steal your thunder."

"Maybe," LidleLin nodded, now kicking around some dirt with her tiny foot, "but I gotta admit there was some sincerity in her voice. Like she admired my victory, even if it were a ruse."

Shady would've shook his head if it weren't embedded into the tree trunk. "It's no wonder no one from any of the other nearby towns will hire any of our young people except for espionage, sabotage and 'finish us off' corporative suicide attempts."

LidleLin sighed, the anger leaving her mind and now being replaced with the depression. "I wish I could've swat that butterfly lie with my sunfly swatter. Why didn't I bring my swatter to town?"

Shady said some other nice cliché friendly encouragements

but LidleLin was thinking hard and reminded herself that she did in fact win the Brain Cleaver Clever Competition contest fair and square and thus had the brain power to think her way out of...

"I'm going to remove that butterfly lie from the nest!" LidleLin proclaimed while performing a leap of preemptive triumph.

Shady and the tree he was stuck in quit breathing and photosynthesizing respectively. "No one's ever removed a butterfly from the collective thought nest" he reminded his friend. "The best you can hope for is a sending another butterfly in to cover the one you don't like."

"No, I don't want that because the butterfly lie will still be under the truthful one. One never can completely obscure the other."

Shady scrunched his eyebrows around the idea, considering what his friend was about to undertake. "Well, I don't think it's a great idea but if you're gonna do it, I advise you visit ConHerm the Wizardist up in the Hep Neck Trash Tree. He might be able to assist ya, my sweet LidleLin."

LidleLin went to where her friend had directed and sure enough after looking way way up, saw a tree full of trash. There were tires, plastic sacks, old machines and many more aesthetically unpleasant rubbish well placed throughout the branches. The only trouble was the blamblue ladder must've grown quite a bit since last time Shady had visited (probably before the whole gettin'-left-in-a-tree-crook thing). Though the blamblue grew out of the ground, the lowest rung was too high up for LidleLin to reach, in spite of her repeated leaping.

"Well, broken baby fingers!" LidleLin cursed, plopping down on the ground in frustration.

Now I need to tell you that LidleLin was normally a calm, disciplined girl and on her wildest days maybe quirky. But in this story you've heard her curse and stomp and kick and I'm sure she'll get around to some other physical and verbal violence. To go from the high of working for years and winning a competition to then having it's legitimacy stolen by a simple sentence utterance, well, it's quite the emotional roller coaster, I think you'd agree. So please give our little friend the benefit of the doubt.

After a good this-day-is-against-me sigh, LidleLin again tried to encourage herself with memories of past triumphs. She thought back to the one time she was passing through a grazing field on her way to the Skifoot Narry Pass, which was blocked by a bitter, old milkless cowcroaker who had divorced 'loving life' and was now having an lusty love affair with 'spite'. LidleLin tried arguing with it, running around it, sweet talking it, kicking it in it's floppy empty utters — all to no avail. Finally she worked with it's stubbornness and proclaimed she didn't want to go through the narry pass anymore but just wanted to look at it. So every angle she tried to glance at the pass, the cowcroaker would do anything to block her way, including at one point standing up on it's tippy toes and waving it's webbed hoofs like a traffic director. She slowly inched back into the shade of a pile of cowcroaker chips (bitter ones, no doubt) and laid down, all while the cowcroaker continued to block her view to the Skifoot Pass. Eventually because it was out in the sun, parts of the animals started to sizzle, at which LidleLin began to eat. In time she had eaten enough of the cranky animal to incapacitate it's impeding behavior and through the narry pass she strolled, a smile resting on her face and full belly resting on her hips.

Now encouraged by her own past triumphs, LidleLin unsuccessfully tried to take a bite out of the blamblue ladder, after which she tried to boil them down to a softer still-unedible consistency after setting a rain cloud on fire, which caused the blamblue to get doused with scalding water. Next, LidleLin decided to go find someone else who might could have better luck eating the ladder.

Ya'll know already that the one creature on any given planet that eats raw hard blamblue are pitpan bears, be they beautiful or dirty and unattractive. So off LidleLin went to attempt to employ the dirty fur bags she saw down the turnpike.

When she got there, the three bears were surrounding a Boarder Hoarder B-Boy Bird, twisting his wing to cough up the nubs of cigarette butts that he had collected to impress a potential feathered girlfriend with a nasty smoking habit.

LidleLin skipped up and danced around, smacking the pitpan bears in the backs of their heads.

"Ya'll outta be ashamed of yourselves" LidleLin chided as the harassed bird flew away from the stunned bears. "What happened in your lives that lead you to harassing birds for belly trash?"

The first pitpan bear seemed to have a abnormally large backside, but upon closer inspection LidleLin realized he was wearing a diaper panted the color of his fur ("Do you know how much time we waste walking to a so-called 'proper' restroom?", he was often heard saying to anyone who would listen, which were usually only slow mountains and quadriplegics).

The second pitpan bear was missing part of an ear and chunks of fur, one exposed part of his hide featuring a tattoo reading, "I own this arm — Affectionally, Peloki the Hammer Wielding ReidDier

The third pitpan bear appeared to have stopped cleaning his nose. Actually it was so caked with crust statues, LidleLin questioned whether he had ever cleaned it and wondered when was the last he'd used it to breathe.

The first unattractive pitpan bear — called Eeee — replied, "When I was young, I chose not to listen to the advice of my parents. They told me to save my money, be kind to others and work hard. It was my opinion that my parents were big boring losers, so why would I listen to them? Hence, I spent money as soon as I got in in my paws, punched people in the face to get more money and laid around staring at my paws until I needed to punch people in the face again.

"Well, eventually people started punching me back, come to find out to make my muscle more tender because they were planning to make burgers out of me.

"Yeah, so I ran away and met these guys doing exotic dancing at a zoo for low income children."

The second unattractive pitpan bear — named Are — reported, "I gotta say, I did listen to my parents. They told me I was smarter and better than everyone else, and if it feels good, I should do it. Which pretty much lead me to the conclusion that my parents were also losers. So I punched them in the face and took their money. That felt good!

"But because of some of the 'feel good' part, I know several little pitpan bears who look like me and are searching for me to punch me in the face for money. Also, I now have certain itches that hurt to scratch. Anyway, I'm hiding in this terrible town until those baby pitpans give up looking for me."

The third unattractive pitpan bear — Senny — said, "Well,

I didn't do what my parents said but I didn't listen to them either, because they really didn't say much of anything. I figured since they were such bad parents, my luck was sure to be better in the world and maybe even brother nature would do me a solid since it gypped me with bad parents and owed me something fierce. So I never punched people in the face but I did complain and whine to everyone until they did give me money to stop whining. And I laid around eating fried onions, smoking cigarettes and staring at my paws until I ran out of those items and realized it was time to put my complainy pants back on.

"That said..." and he actually walked over to a plastic sack full of nasty, smelly cloths and pulled out a particular pair of pants, putting them on (well, kinda — he only put one leg in and was too lazy to put the other leg in). "Do you think you could help a pitpan bear down on his luck? I never stood a chance in life! I mean look at my pants..."

LidleLin waved away the pitpan bears' pathetic stories, "Holy hot dumpster gelatin! You let those boring stories ruin ya'll's lives? Brother!

"So yeah, follow me today and I'll give you at least something proper for a pitpan bear to eat."

The dirty and unattractive pitpan bears gladly ate enough of the blamblue ladder so LidleLin could reach the rungs (although they never stopped complaining about empty coin purses and of having nicotine withdrawals).

The tiny girl got up to the conjurer hermit who was quite surprised to have a visitor, having not had any in a while who couldn't fly or didn't have stilt legs. But quickly getting down to business, LidleLin laid out what she was after.

"Hmmm…", ConHerm thought, rubbing his stale-food fortified beard, "I'm thinking maybe of a soul-transferrence procedure, where I could swap your spirit with some creature that's small enough to get up in the memory nest."

The man looked to LidleLin who just flipped her hands and added, "Yeah, ok, however! Let's get to it, Dr. Foodbeard!"

ConHerm didn't quite know why the girl thought his name was Foodbeard but reminded himself that paying customers never really needed to know his correct name.

So he had LidleLin sit on his transference high chair rig and then put his pet dairy dragonfly in the other tiny high chair. And within a few minutes the two spirits were switched and with what could be counted as a wave goodbye by one of the dairy dragonfly arms, LidleLin — in insect form — zoomed out the conjurer's window.

I didn't mention this before because it wasn't relevant but beings now that it is, I must tell you that LidleLin is nothing short than a cutie. And ConHerm couldn't help but be constantly noticing this as this body that now was inhabited by an insect soul looked around, as if it were looking for where it's wings were.

And the tinker began to get notions...

LidleLin as the dairy dragonfly approached the floating memory nest and without delay shot right in behind another butterfly in through one of the nest doors. And there it was, the glowing, twitching and at times fluttering ball that was the people's collective memory, made entirely of butterflies. Some were freshly bright colored and others were faded to that of drab colored moths. There were even some that were so frail that they now had dusty skeletal webs of what once were wings.

It didn't take long for LidleLin to find the lie about her — it was still busily flapping, it's colors pulsing with each flap on wings that seemed to have been growing.

"Unbrushed dynomitosaur teeth!" LidleLin exclaimed in her dairy dragonfly mind. "I bet that mom of Snippy is still nursing lies and unfounded theories as I hover here! Well, not for long!"

And with that, without even thinking why, LidleLin ate the butterfly lie, head, body, wings and all.

"That were surprisingly delicious!" she exclaimed as she savored the lepidoptera aftertaste.

"Hmmm...what other untrue treats do we have here?"

ConHerm hopped off the last ladder rung for the first time in many many years.

"Wow, this floor sure is stable!" the conjurer commented referring to the ground.

Close behind him was the dairy dragonfly minded LidleLin body, slowly descending while every few moments trying to twitch it's back.

"Come on dear, they're not there" ConHerm reminded the dairy dragonfly mind. "You have much more useful and beautiful legs now. Come, let's use them to parade around town now."

Shady existed in his sedimentary stance as he almost always had in his life. But he began to have second thought regrets about sending his best friend up to the wizard. The scientist, although having a great reputation for results, did not in turn have a good reputation for ethics. For example, he once fascinated a spout on a cuddle slug's head and told it that it was pregnant. The wizard had figured out that the cuddle slug's brain makes a particular chemical when it thinks it's going to pop one out. This particular chemical ConHerm drained via the spout and then sold as a potion to sock knitting factories, that in turn gave it to it's workers, increasing productivity by 200%. Sadly, the slug became very depressed when it found out the truth and began to overeat and lurk about nurseries, creeping out babies far and wide. It was attacked by a militia of Salty

Cracker Skate Boarders and died a gooey, childless death. The wizard just found another cuddle slug and continued to make bank until that one went on a dirty diaper stealing spree. And so the cycle went on.

Yes, the wizardist had done many incredible things "without the shackles of kitchen light conscience", as he had put it (a lot of people didn't get his meaning but ConHerm later clarified he was referring to cock roaches' fear of the kitchen light. ConHerm needed a better publicist, many mused) and this is what worried Shady the most.

The embedded boy's regret turned into fevered frenzy at the thought of what ConHerm might be justifying at that moment with his best friend, Lidlelin.

It was then that Shady got some life-changing notions...

LidleLin's thorax was about to burst, she'd eaten so many butterfly memories. It was difficult to stop herself because there so many lies but also opinions and slants on the truth in the collective memory that she'd always wished didn't exist. Also her dairy dragonfly mouth found the beautiful insects incredibly delicious!

"Uh!" she exclaimed patting her belly. "Mission accomplished, my little odonata friend. As soon as I have a rest, I'll get your body back to ya and I'll be basking in the truth."

Well, in the town new lies were being spun at that very moment, except that Snippy's mom were not the culprit this time around.

ConHerm strolled proudly through the sale aisle of the town's MegaSuperDuperpooper Market with pretty LidleLin the body hanging on his arm. In her limited insect understanding, the cute girl grinned admiringly at the conjurer's verbal crumbs of debonair plaid particle wit and cave squishies chemistry facts. It was the peak going-home-from-work-to-pick-a-few-things-and-avoid-my-bleak-home-life-for-a-few-minutes-more time of the day, so the places were jammed with buying hands and the staring eyes that went with them. The people there all stopped their browsing through the racks of cloths, clutter and comrades to take in the very unlikely sight.

The conjurer took it all in matter of factly, pretending to sort through some discounted dehydrated brain picture frames, glancing up occasionally to make a comment to his adorable companion about structure quality and the public's general ignorance about all things synapse, and then would look up pleasantly surprised at all the gaping mouths.

This occurrence went on at every other major public purchasing place that afternoon, ConHerm parading around with his beautiful bug brained girlfriend, not buying a single solitary item. The butterfly lies flew up as thick hairy bat clouds.

"Hey guys!" Shady called out at the dirty and unattractive pitpan bears wandering by, looking for a place to sleep off their ladder consumption.

Are crinkled his scarred nose at the tree with the face in it. "Whoa!"

"Hey do think ya'll can help me out with something?" the tree face posed.

"You got any money?" Eeee asked.

The face said nothing but looked sad.

"How about weapons?" asked Are. "We're thinking of highjacking a revolution so we don't have to work anymore."

The face looked sadder.

Senny sighed. "Cigarettes, at least?"

The tree face lit up!

"Where's the swill grill spill is my body!", a tiny voice hollered out of a certain tree filled with trash.

"Which color do you like Lovey Honey Face?" ConHerm asked the body of LidleLin while in the Fancy Shmancy

Dress Troff women's fashion shop. The girl shrugged, not knowing what 'color' was, much less what the conjurer was saying.

"LidleLin!" said a same-aged girl that walked up to the two. This girl kinda stood out because she wore thin summer shorts and blouse, yet also a wintertime scarf.

"I'm so glad I found you! I want to totally apologize for my mother and her big bleepin' mouth. She speaks without knowing what the bleep she's saying. Well, that's not true — she knows exactly what she's saying: she's a manipulative hydrant sniffer! I should know — she's begin manipulating my life ever since I fell out of her body, threatening to withhold her mammary milk unless I smiled at her like she was the best thing since baked foot bean bread.

"Anyway, I just want you to know that I know you won the competition fair and square. You're more clever than me and my conniving mother put together, and that's saying something! My mother gave ear lobe rubs to all the judges the night before and left hunks of raw cookie globs in all their mailboxes the morning of.

"Anyway, I plan on telling everyone I know the truth — heck I might even get a shirt made saying as much! Do you want one? Oh — naw, that'd be weird, I guess, wearing a shirt proclaiming your own superiority. Plus it looks like your grandpa here's gonna buy a nice dress for ya.

"Okay, I hope we can be friends after all this" the girl

obviously named Snippy said as she embraced LidleLin's body. "Heck lecky weck — maybe we can form a super truth telling team to battle my mother!"

And at that, the verbose girl bounced off down the pinafore aisle. ConHerm had no idea what all that blather was about but knew he was very much bothered by the "grandpa" comment.

"I think the HelpMeForgetMyLife juice store is up over here" Eeee said.

"Dude, I'm starving!" Are complained.

"We just ate!" Eeee countered. "Plus Senny is having nicotine withdrawals! The sooner we get back to the trash tree house and find that hyper girl, the sooner we get our cigarettes from the talking tree."

Senny looked very irritated, which is hardly noticeable to other non-pitpan bears, the bears looking so comatose all the time. But in fact he was about to rip a crying baby's head off, try to smoke it's full diaper and then drink it's crying baby blood.

"Hey pitpan bears!" hollered a teeny tiny voice.

"What the dinner bell was that?" asked Are.

"I think it was that dairy dragonfly in front of us" observed Eeee.

"Ah thank Brother Nature!" proclaimed Senny. "I smoked one of those things once and you'd be surprised how it will calm ya the plump glump down! Someone grab it for me!"

"Come on Senny, we can light up some real cigarettes if we do what the tree with the face asked us" Eeee tried to persuade.

"Pitpan bears! It's me — LidleLin!"

"No it's not!" Senny countered.

"Yeah — dairy dragonfly's can't talk!" Are added.

"Plus we just saw LidleLin with her old timey boyfriend over at the Frozen Hot Girl Spit Sickle Stand" Eeee reminded.

"So yeah, you can't be LidleLin or talking" Are concluded for the three.

"Ya know," Senny thought aloud, "I can smoke both this dairy dragonfly and then the tree guy's cigarettes so I don't see why ya'll have to make this an 'either/or' situation."

"Pitpan bears! I fed you a ladder earlier today!" the flying bug proclaimed.

At this, maybe the pitpan bears reconsidered their stance on talking dairy dragonflies, smoking dairy dragonflies and other closely held beliefs. Or maybe they were so confused they just quit arguing to let their brains heal.

ConHerm was addicted to the attention he was getting. There were a few reasons he'd become a hermit so many years ago and one of those reasons was that not many folks paid him any mind. Well, that was changing today, even if it was all a matter of pretense. It made these gaspers all the more the suckas they deserved to be. ConHerm was playin' them like a cowcroaker gut fiddle.

"Oh, this is deliciously interesting!" Snippy's mom exclaimed to herself and anyone in earshot. Her eyes were on ConHerm strutting in front of the courthouse, his arm around LidleLin not anything like a grandfather would to his granddaughter. He actually was carrying her, one would find under closer inspection. The girl was clearly his love interest, or at least that's what Mrs. Plyers concluded, again both internally and audibly. "I might've been more right about LidleLin than I realized! Repeat something long enough and it eventually comes true, that's what I always say." For good measure and comedy, she repeated that phrase several times. And there they went — more butterfly lies up to the sky.

In that strange way that little meanies' mind do, Mrs. Plyers was racing to think of any old men that might want to court Snippy when that train of thought was interrupted by three sad looking pitpans running past, chasing a dairy dragonfly it seemed.

"Boy, those pitpan bears must either be hungry or on drugs!" Mrs. Plyers proclaimed, unleashing another flapping memory.

But then the dairy dragonfly dove into ConHerm's face, causing the old man to drop LidleLin on the ground like a baby doll full of sand. Senny shoved the wizard on the ground and began searching the scientists' pockets for cigs or cash. The other two pitpan bears picked up LidleLin, dropped her a few times more before they were able to get a better hold of the girl. After the pick pocketing pitpan bear finished his search, he twisted the scientist's arm to a painful angle and forced him to come along.

As the bears and insect went buzzing back past Mrs. Plyers, the mother thought she heard the dairy dragonfly say something about maybe not having a body to go back to if the pitpan bears handled it too much more.

Snippy's mom shook her head trying to piece together what had happened but didn't get very far in those thought processes either because she next thought she saw a tree riding in the back of a taxi.

LidleLin the dragon fly and the pitpan bears (with ConHerm and LidleLin the body in their scruffy arms) arrived at the bottom of the trash tree house, just about to get up the ladder to make everything right. But wouldn't ya know it — Eeee had been doin' some thinking and after he dropped LidleLin the body on the ground, called over his dirty and unattractive brothers to him.

"I've been doin' some figurin'," he whispered, "and the way I see it, we could really come out ahead if we actually took some initiative for once."

"What do ya got?" sniffed Are jonesin' for a load of baked foot bean bread right about then.

"Hey what are you chumps doin' down there?" LidleLin the dairy dragonfly demanded from up in the trash tree lab. "Why is my body layin' in the dirt?"
The scheming pitpan bear began confiding as quickly as he could. By the time LidleLin the dairy dragonfly had dropped back down to earth, the mutiny was already in motion.

"It's like this, LidleLin" Eeee the ring leader explained, "we've made a deal with the scientist here to keep full use of your body however he sees fit and in exchange, he'll invent stuff for us. Like a girl made of regenerating blamblue!"

"Or a gelephant that sneezes gold snot!" Are added

"And a cigarette butt maker" Senny suggested.

"Why not a whole cigarette maker, Senny?" Eeee posed. "You gotta think bigger now."

"Yes, it's gonna be great!" Senny conceded at the prospects.

"But ConHerm can't just pull those kind of things out of his butt!" LidleLin pleaded.

"Yes I can!" the conjurist countered, holding his eyeglasses up to his backside. "Even my butt is super smart, my new pitpan friends!"

"You guys are idiots!" LidleLin the dairy dragonfly proclaimed while dropping to the ground and stomping it with her tiny little insect feet. "What makes you think ConHerm's not going to double-cross ya'll like he did me? What if you wake up with your mind inside a turd that just came out of this conjurer's super smart arse, havin' to watch your real pitpan bear body gettin' all kissed on by this crusty old sneak perve?"

The pitpan bears all scratched their mangy heads, obviously not having thought out the whole strategy too far ahead.

"Well, well well!" proclaimed Snippy's mom saddling up to the scene. "LidleLin's so tired from all her old man lovin' that she's taking a nap on the ground!"

More butterflies flew up into the collective conscious nest, which prompted another insect foot stomp.

The confusion was all the time the scientist needed. ConHerm grabbed LidleLin the body and scurried up the ladder, struggling with some of the rungs which had which a variety of bite marks and missing chunks. And this was all the time a certain fellow stuck in a tree needed.

Jumping out of the taxi (after paying the driver of course, who luckily agreed to accept as currency a bird's nest, a kite and a kitten skeleton), Shady babbled something in tree-speak to the tree that ConHerm was climbing into. His foliaged brother shuddered, which shook not only the ladder off the tree but showered the ground with tons of trash, including a tree house lab. Some key pieces of trash (a sap bucket and a petrified cloud) nailed two of the three pitpan bears in their noggins and a falling LidleLin the body almost squashed LidleLin the insect, if were not the quick branch action of Shady. In a nice pause, the embedded fellow glanced lovingly at LidleLin the dairy dragonfly on one limb and LidleLin the girl on another. There was also ConHerm in another catching branch but Shady promptly let that appendage go as limp as boiled noodle, letting the wizard's super smart butt land on the last standing dirty and unattractive pitpan bear.

Snippy's mom was strangely umbrelled from the raining rubbish by all the butterfly lies she was running with in her mind about how she was going to spin all of this to the rest of the community. Still, her lying couldn't protect her from the passionate anger of Shady and immediately found herself with a mouth full of twigs. Making sure her mom wouldn't hurt anymore folks for a while, Snippy strolled up to the scene and tied her wintertime scarf around her mom's head to keep the twigs in tight. The daughter's bare neck exposed, everyone quietly took note of the multitude of tattooed butterflies on the girl's beautiful nape, all in the middle of tattooed gun cross hairs.

LidleLin the dairy dragonfly danced on one of Shady's branches in joy before buzzing up to her friend's face and giving it a tiny sweet kiss.

"How did you get here?" the bug asked her hero.

"By taxi, but before that I found myself missing and being so worried about you I couldn't help but uproot myself to find you!"

That got the face in the tree another insect kiss.

To wrap it all up, ConHerm was persuaded to find through his wrecked home the contraptions to put the right souls in the right bodies.

The dirty and unattractive pitpan bears decided to break up the band and go their separate ways. Funny thing is, they all got the same idea and went back to their families. Eeee's family was glad to have their son back and quickly got him back on the right track. Are and Senny didn't fair so well in that neither family were that excited to see them. So in time, the two crappy pitpan bears ran into each other, got so desperate they allowed themselves to be completely shaved and began modeling for sleazy sculptors. They did hatch a scheme together that was sure to make them big time money but it failed because they got sick from being hairless and kept coughing and hacking as they tried to rob a lava jewelry shop, no one quite understanding what the bears were demanding. The owner of the shop took them to the hospital, he felt so sorry for them.

In the end, they ended up back on the turnpike doing the same ol' same.

It was often claimed by some folks in the town that they saw a dairy dragonfly jetting around in cute skirts. And it was true; the bug had gotten accustomed to the fashion while in LidleLin's body. It never did develop a taste for amorous old shriveled men and so continued to have a policy of only dating other dairy dragonflies.

LidleLin and Shady became girlfriend and boyfriend and Snippy their closest friend. The three improved on their studies together, during the hot days never having to look for shelter from the sun. Although it took a while, LidleLin lovingly pulled at her tree boyfriend's bark, and later at his wood insides until eventually he was looking less and less like a tree and was able to get through normal sized doorways. He always had a woody outside but that was ok for the time being — LidleLin loved his sawdust scent and would etch adoring woods into his chest/trunk.

"By the way," LidleLin asked one day as she and Shady were watching a dull dirt puppet play about a sapling in a saw mill, "I've always wondered, what did you send the pitpan bears into town that day for?"

"Oh yeah," the tree boy said scrunching his face, "I'd sent them to strong arm a scroll publishing company into offering ConHerm a writing contract. My hope was in how most academic types that write do, he'd publish one of his theories before it was thoroughly proven and out of pride stick to his literary guns, even after some other younger conjurer proved him incorrect. That would sink his credibility and thus leave him bankrupt and mentally destroyed, perfectly ripe to defeated by you, if need be."

"Dang, Shady!" LidleLin's mouth exploded in amusement, "Not exactly the most speediest plan I've ever heard. My body might've been his child bride many times over by the time your scheme would've reached fruition!"

"Yeah," Shady nodded, if he could've, "it was a slow burner."

Snippy's mom didn't quit her low down ways and in fact amped them up as soon as she undid her mouth, trying to save face. But, as LidleLin finally accepted, people are gonna believe what they want to believe and if it's lies, that's their problem. What most don't know is that butterfly lies also sneak back down to the ground at night, and into the believer's heads while they sleep, pushing buttons, shifting gears and ripping out mind wiring. Electric volcanos erupt on the brain, which lead to destructive behavior on the part of the lie believers, initially to others but always eventually to themselves. Mrs. Plyers eventually ended up falling in love with Senny, whom just rolled her into a blanket and smoked her alive.

With no lab or home, ConHerm answered an advertisement for a Brother Nature cult off in another city. The fanatics wanted some scientists to validate their sincere beliefs that when people plowed the land to grow food or flowers, the planet cried. Even ConHerm thought these people were nuts but wizards have to eat. So he augmented the claims that quakes were the planet shuddering in pain and that if folks just quit farming, the tremors would stop forever. Luckily, half the cult lost interest after their trust funds ran out and other half were swallowed by a big crevice during an quake. ConHerm started yet another new life in another place and eventually convinced a magistrate to allow the conjurer to legally marry a molecule. That was a weird wedding night, I was told. The patrons in the motel rooms surrounding the scientist's complained about the strange noises that persisted all...night...long. One might say infinitely.

Eventually LidleLin, Shady and Snippy moved away together to find their fortunes where there was more opportunity for people of merit. This didn't go well at first because no one would give the people from Winkyburg a fair chance. So they eventually just quit saying where they were from and in time excelled in their individual dream jobs from their hard work and integrity.

One last thing, at the end of time, Fuchin the Maker entered the collective memory house and set the butterflies aflame, the lies burning away but the true ones remaining unconsumed, and forever staying fiery truths. Everything wrong and out of place was forgotten forever.

Wink and Marble Proof

Recognizing a name on one of the letters in it's bosom, the mailbox dreaded opening it's mouth for it's owner. The name on the dunler tree leaf envelope was never good.

Wink, a tiger, when he finally got out to the post box, sighed seeing the name and slowly trotted back to his house, ready to have the rest of the day ruined.

"Dear Cousin", the tiger read to himself at his kitchen table, *"I hope you are well and I truly regret that I only seem to write when I'm trouble."* Wink moaned at the insincerity of his kin's words.

His cousin SlipStep was one of those souls whom worked very hard to avoid working. One letter ago the cousin cat was asking for money to buy a prosthetic body, as that he'd wagered his own on a behind-the-barn cowcroaker race. Lucky Fat Chance was beat by every other contestant, including Bulbous Slouch, Frunck Envasun Yawn and Yip Yip Sluggy Clip (the latter not even having all it's original legs). The bookies removed his head as SlipStep was trying to sneak away dressed as a pile of hay and the thugs used the rest of him to line the inside of their steam engine good time van.

Two letters ago the cousin was asking for a letter validating that he was an dribble-drooling idiot so that a charity would give him money set aside especially for dribble-drooling idiots.

So Wink continued reading with a mix of dread and curiosity of what kind of creative trouble his cousin was in now.

"I find myself writing this letter from within the bowels of an Uh Oh monster. It's a long story but the short of it is that I got eaten near the Great Hip Shaking Vine of Ami and some of the larger bacteria in the creature have renounced Brother Nature, embraced Makerism and currently run a postal service for all those here waiting to be digested. Most of my roommates are writing to confess their sins, complete their wills and say their goodbyes to loved ones. I am writing to ask if you might try to get me out of here. Some of the Uh Oh's bile poured into our holding gullet chamber when the monster was seemingly doing a cartwheel and some the acidic slush splattered on my ear. It hurt *very much bad and I can't imagine the rest of my limited body enduring a whole pool of it.*

"Hope to hear from you soon. Maybe not your favorite cousin, but most definitely your most not-boring cousin, SlipStep."

Tiger put down the letter and laid his head on the table. He would never let any other creature catch him doing this but he was truly defeated by the thought of how foolish this one family member was.

Wink put some dishes in the sink and stared out the kitchen window, thinking about the situation. Brother Nature would say let his cousin go the way of all the rest of sick and stupid creatures. The Maker would say he should go try to save the pathetic guy. Tiger Wink wasn't much of a fan of either schools of thought, but one or the other of the choices was all he had.

It was at this moment that he finally noticed that a rabbit was in his backyard staring at a water piper sticking out of the ground. The tiger watched the fluffy creature for a few minutes and nothing happened. He thought about going out and asking what the animal was doing on his property but the thought bored him, rabbits never being very good conversationalists. He actually found most of them rude, they rarely answering any of your questions, seemingly so concentrated on vigorously trying to make something fall out of their noses by all that twitching they do.

A couple days passed with still no resolve about what to do about his cousin. "If the weather is nice, maybe I'll go rescue SlipStep" the tiger decided to himself. Looking out his window again, after he found the weather was overcast, he also noticed that there the rabbit still sat. It was at this point that that Wink realized the bunny might actually be dead. So he pulled a pan and big metal spoon out of his cabinet, opened the window and banged as if it were the new year. The rabbit remained unmoved and the tiger sighed, a little sad for both the stupid dead animal and the fact he would have to dispose of the body later if he didn't want his window view spoiled by a fluffy rotting carcass.

But instead of doing this deed, the tiger hoped very intently that some beast that loved already dead things would eat it for him.

But well you know, the next day, Wink looked out his window for another weather check and there the rabbit still sat, dead as a crippled stone at the bottom of a well.

The tiger sighed and went to look for his shovel.

The big cat began digging the hole as close to the rabbit as possible without chopping the thing with the blade, so he could just simply knock the corpse in the hole and be done with it.

Hole dug, Wink lifted the shovel to tap the dead critter. It was then that he heard a carefully worded, "Please...don't...do...that."

The tiger crinkled his eyes. "You mean you're not dead?"

"Not yet but...I might be soon...if this scoundrel of a water pipe...has it's way."

Wink shook his head. "Care to expound?"

"Can't you see, cat? I'm having a stand off ....with this menace...this deadly carrier of liquid!"

The tiger was tempted to just go back in the house and do something more productive than converse with this lunatic. But he had to admit the cracked nut in his yard was infinitely more interesting than anything currently residing in his quiet, peaceful home.

"Well, if you weren't emerged in your staring contest, you could see my confused face and you'd know that I indeed do not 'see'. School me, rabbit."

"What school did you go to, big kitty? One where at the graduation ceremony you were handed your certificate and if you didn't eat it, you didn't have to return the next year?"

"You know I could eat you in one swallow?"

"Yes but eating me wouldn't help you understand the seriousness of this water pipe, now would it?"

"Listen rabbit, I've known this water pipe longer than you, I'm guessing. We've been neighbors for many years and we've lived in complete peace. True it never asks me how I'm doing or waves when I come home, but neither do I. We live in harmonious indifference."

The rabbit made a shameful clicking noise. "The oldest trick in the book. Giving the appearance of peace and harmony all while grooming it's war machine. One day you'll wake up in your bed and you head's no longer attached to your body!"

This reminded Wink of his cousin. He sighed bored and depressed and was no longer interested with the foolish rodent.

"Okay Rabbit. Good luck with your battle here. I'm going inside. Dinner's at sun down. Come on in if you get hungry."

The tiger took a bowl off his dinner table and approached the stove, dipping out some gelephant soup out of a pot. Chasing the animal that became this meal brought Wink a slight grin. The gelephant is a giant fierce creature, more times than not eating anything that cared to challenge it. But given it's skin, muscle and organs are as transparent as jellyfishes', you can totally see what the beast has just eaten. So if you happened to catch one that had just gulped down a citrusy bone hair goat or a gaggle of salty lurky turkeys, well the chance of tasting that delectable harmony was worth the risk of being digested oneself.

So the tiger smiled more as he looked forward to his triumphantly quiet meal and felt gracious enough to maybe consider a response to his SlipStep's letter. But when he turned to face the table, there the rabbit sat, looking starved and defeated.

They ate in mostly silence but eventually Tiger brought up

the last question he had about their whole chance meeting. "So, who put you up to fighting the water pipe?"

The rabbit (Marble Proof, his name come to find out) nibbled and swallowed. "A monk — my abbot at the monastery."

Tiger nodded. "Mmm...sounds like something a monk would do."

"Not a fan of monks?"

"They're not all bad. I just have had issues with most of them."

They continued to eat in silence, Wink forgetting about the rabbit and looking back up at his cousin's letter pinned to the flower print wallpapered wall.

Then he said, "Listen Rabbit, if you want to be of some help and fight a real menace, why don't you join me to try to help a guy I know out of an acidic jam."

Marble Proof chewed at what meat was still in his mouth, studied the tiger for a second and then nodded with the most nobility a rabbit can.

"So how long you been domesticated?" the rabbit posed to the tiger on a path, a day into their journey.

The Tiger grinned a little. "Since my early days of adulthood."

"How that'd come about, can I ask?"

The Tiger sighed. "Sure. I came home one day from a hunt, my wife and cubs were missing. There were signs of a fight and so I tracked down whatever had taken them. Long story short, I caught up with a gunkswoller and gave it the fight of his life.

"The thing was much fiercer than I but I knew he'd killed my family and really was just trying to end my own pointless life while going out with some vindication.

"Anyway, a human showed up with a similar grievance with the inconsiderate beast and we fought the gunkswoller together. We killed the thing, though by the end of the fight, I was severely injured." Tiger pointed at his perpetually shut eye.

"The human carried me to his home, pulled the monster's claw out of my eye socket, patched me up and took care of me until I was healed. We became friendly, one night we even crying together about the horror of finding our loved one's bones in the gunkswoller's stool. After I got better, I found I had a taste for living in a house and standing on all twos."

"So, you like humans?"

"Not the ones who act like animals but the rest of them, yes."

A few hours later, the two were walking away from a small town pushing a wheelbarrow containing a few honey suckle glazed fried butter babies they had just purchased.

The tiger turned the rabbit's questioning around. "How long you been tame?"

Marble Proof began to shake something out of his nose while relaying, "A gang of little boys on wooden tricycles were initiating a new member and made him do a drive-by marble sling attack while I was dinning at a local human garden. He nailed me in the head real good!" The hare pulled back some fur, highlighting a big dent in his skull.

"The newbie gangsta must've felt bad for putting me in a coma, came back, stuck me in a dandelion jelly jar and left me on a trailer doorstep at the Shaolin Salvage Yard. The junk monks nursed me back to health and taught me their many ways."

"Oh," replied Wink chuckling,"you mean like their fine-tuned methods of battling water pipes?"

Marble Proof was silent, brooding on that whole confusing episode.

The tiger hesitated but continued. "I probably shouldn't

spoil you all the fun of becoming enlightened by their mind numbingly boring methods but I'm pretty sure it's some kind of rump-backwards riddle."

"Hunh?"

Wink shook his head. "The pipe isn't really a villain. You probably were just supposed to stare at it until you nearly starved to death and then you'dve gained some personal insight, thank the water pipe, bow to it, hug it or something equally nonsensical."

"I don't understand" the rabbit said in a very worried tone. "Why would the abbott play a trick on me?"

"Well, now you know why I'm not fond of most monks. I mean, don't take it personal. They do it to everybody, although the Salvage Order are not as cruel as some of the other monks in this world. Most monks just sit there rocking and humming while the world get pillaged and raped. At least your order have given their lives to defend the weak with their foot kicks and finger flicks."

Marble Proof didn't take refuge in Wink's respectable distinction between the various orders of monks. He just sighed so hurt. "I was willing to die to take that pipe down..."

"Hmmm..." Tiger said nodding as they approached a group of humans sticking out if for anything their many hand telescopes and super fancy cloths that were trying to be passed off as casual.

"Stop Tiger!", said the one with the biggest telescope, eyeing the wheelbarrow's contents. "Do you plan on harming the Oh Uh Individual with that fried butter baby?"

Tiger laughed. "If I were, I wouldn't tell you bunch."

The bunch in question huddled, talking amongst themselves about what to do with this verbally elusive beast. Obviously they came to a conclusion, indicated by their spokesperson addressing the Tiger again.

"Since you refuse to answer our feverish questioning, we are going to assume you mean our big beloved friend harm!"

"Who the heck in your neck are these people?", Marble Proof asked Wink.

"Very rich and hence bored people who call themselves the Oh Uh Activists. Everyone else calls them the Oh Brother Idiots. Regardless of their name, they follow the Oh Uh monster around, to both watch it eat others and to also protect it from souls like us."

"Oh" the rabbit said not amused. "Yet another counter natural denomination of the Brother Nature Cult."

"You're planning your strategy, yes?" another one of the Oh Brother Idiots asked the travelers.

"Maybe" the tiger responded. "Hey, why don't you give us a riddle or something, and if we get it right, you let us kill your pet monster."

"It's not a monster!" screamed one activist.

"Yes, you are the monsters!" declared another.

"Listen," Wink replied, "it ate my cousin."

"Brother Nature has ordained it to eat those that are not meant to live!" countered another.

"Actually, I don't doubt that my cousin should've been eaten" agreed the tiger. "But if I kill the Oh Uh Monster, then by your argument Brother Nature has ordained me to kill it. Ya follow?"

This stumped them. And as Oh Brother Idiots argued amongst themselves, Wink and Marble Proof waltzed on by.

"They've gotten past us!" realized one of the activists holding up his telescope to spy the two animals not a couple meters away.

At that, the bunch rushed at the tiger and rabbit, brandishing their scopes. But with a quick slice and slash,

Wink shredded their nice dress down clothes until they were left standing in their very pristine white underwear.

Defeated, the Oh Brother Idiots began a mix of wailing for both their clothes and their now endangered favorite animal, consoling each other for these tragedies — both past and coming — and retelling each other how the tiger brutally attacked them.

Getting within smelling range to the Oh Uh Monster, Marble Proof asked Wink, "So, is your cousin tame?"

The tiger shook his head. "Well, he was. He and all my family came to find my hide after the gunkswoller incident and after they kept harassing me about losing my edge, I beat them all up until the saw my domesticated point of view. Now they all drink moon tea and read Oinky Oinky Poetry.

"Anyway, my cousin fell into a bad group of humans that seemed the picture of domestication — sharply dressed, well organized, clever, all that — but they were just well dressed animals, using sway and paperwork instead of claws and teeth to take food out of the mouths of the weak.

"It's been a downhill ever since — downhill and into the waiting room above a belly of an Oh Uh monster."

The rabbit never got much of a chance to consider all this when they came across another bunch of beings.

"Oh, there they are!" Tiger proclaimed looking up ahead.

Marble Proof smiled at a group of odd creatures and surmised, "So the Uh Oh has his own Thick Whisker Follow Feeders!"

"Yes," Wink replied, "the beast is sometimes picky when it raids a village. True, it often just kills everything but after the massacre is complete, it often only likes to eat the babies. When it gets it's fill, it moves on somewhere else to sleep or mate or whatever."

"And that's when these guys move in for the crumbs."

"Yes, big chunky, bloody crumbs."

Thick Whisker Follow Feeders can't talk like the Idiots. So when they saw the tiger and the rabbit together, they assumed the obvious, and thus came projectile whiskers blazing.

"I got this" Marble Proof said casually to his companion. And from his traveling sack pulled out some weapons the tiger could see was forged from briar switches.

"Attention, my fellow beings!" the rabbit addressed the approaching Feeders. "Here's a point in your life that you can change course — you can either stop feeding off people's tragedy and misery or, partake in the feast of tragedy and misery yourself."

The on rushers neither slowed or gave any other indication they were going to change their life directions.

"Understood" Marble Proof acknowledged.

And with the lighting jumps that only a rabbit that was trained in the art of fighting could exhibit, Marble Proof shot amongst and out of the Thick Whisker Follow Feeders, puncturing and slicing at key points in the their bodies. In a few seconds, they all had collapsed to the ground, in terrible pain and unable to move save twitches.

"Behold the 'Twitching Nose Transference Technique', developed by myself Marble Proof, with the assistance of Sister JooLice", the rabbit proclaimed.

Wink laughed out loud at the sight of all these creature's legs and arms twitching with the fury of his friend's nose.

As the two recommenced their journey, the tiger asked, "Why didn't you just kill them to put them out of their misery? They have no other skills and now no working tendons it seems. They'll probably starve to death."

"Maybe," returned the stoic rabbit, "but every creature I think should be afforded a chance to reflect on their sins and give up their low down ways. I know I would want this if I had made the wrong choices in life, all my life."

"Spoken like a true monk."

"Which reminds me," MarbleProof said with crinkled bunny brows, "what's with all the hatin' on my brothers and sisters?"

Wink sighed. "There's a plethora of reasons but chiefly I just don't think they're the moral masters people see them as and often not much help to the rest of us. Living in the monastery is not particularly noble or difficult. It's a form of running from weakness instead of disciplining one's self from it's power over us. I mean it's easy to be good in a controlled environment. It's far harder to do good where you have actually freedom not to."

Marble Proof nodded in consideration. "Maybe Abbot Mutemi's life story might validate your summary but it also might implore you to see the monks with a little more grace.

"You see, Mutemi was born to parents who didn't want him and treated him with hostility. When he grew older, he met a woman who was kind to him. She was the first person ever kind to him, actually, and so they married. She loved him and was good to him. But one day Mutemi realized he didn't love her the way that a husband should love a wife, because he met briefly another woman whom stirred his heart. He was so drawn to her, his heart pulsed hurt every second he was not in her arms. In their short few minutes together, he laughed as he'd never laughed and saw more color in the world than he'd ever seen before.

"After this, being with his wife was pure misery, not

because he wanted to be with the other woman (which was true) but because, ' With every act of love I accepted from her — from her smiles to her sitting our child in my lap — I swallowed more and more poison trickling from the deceit in my brain. My heart was not hers and every minute I remained with her was a minute more added to the lies numbering in the eons.'

"So tortured by all this, Mutemi fled, not into the arms of the other woman but got a job as an ocean tree arborist . While he attended to the sea seeds, shoots and branches, he reflected on his whole life and realized that even if his parents had not loved him, if they had just took care of him, that would've been better than letting their unwant dictate their cruelty.

"So he attempted to return to his wife but she would not take him back. Apparently the other woman had come around to return to Mutemi a tiny book of his sketches he'd left behind that one day. The wife put two and two together and maybe assumed more had happened than actually had. Nonetheless, she told Mutemi that because of his betrayal, he could never come back and he would never see his child again.

"The abbott decided he had squandered his privilege to live in society and so joined the Salvage Order. He's a terribly likable guy and was promoted to abbot in a few short years. I think he's taken the charred bones of his situation and made crutches out of them."

"I get that" Wink nodded. "So, some of your brothers and sisters are weaker than most. Do they acknowledge this?"

"Not specifically, other than they recognize they are not higher than any other being, righteous or not.

"And really I don't think Abbott Mutemi's weakness has went away. I noticed he was lighting up around one junkess monkess in particular and he must've noticed it himself and so he sent her away on some kind of long term mission."

"Like a mission to have a stand off with a leaf filled gutter."

Marble Proof moaned with a smile. And then returned, "Hey are you trying to say the Abbott has a crush on m-"

At mid-'me', the journey's destination appeared not a few meters in front of them.

"We're here" said Wink.

Marble Proof took in the sight of the terrifyingly large creature, but still got out, "Is this the part where we give it the butter baby?"

The tiger answered by racing the wheelbarrow towards monster as fast as he could. He stopped at the tattered floaty feet of the creature and bounded back to rejoin the rabbit.

And as they expected, the Uh Oh monster bent over to

examine the contraption and it's contents. But not as they expected, the creature took a big swipe at the wheelbarrow, sending the fried butter babies flying through the air. So hard in fact, it is said the delicious treats were seen for miles and attracted the attention of a compassionate skirt maker who raced to catch them, initially beginning to raise them as real children until he realized they were just pastries.

"Uh Oh" said the tiger.

"That wasn't supposed to happen, was it?" asked the rabbit.

"No, it weren't. The monster must've gotten wise that the fried butter babies are a decoy."

"Are you worried?"

"For us, a little. For the rest of the world, a lot. I'd be like one chicken telling all the other chicken in the world, 'Hey, guys — did ya ever wonder why some chickens seem to never come by the house any more and we always find their feathers in a pile behind the barn?'"

"Except this chicken is a infanticidal maniac."

"Exactly."

"Well, maybe our next mission will be that of disinformation among Uh Oh communication lines."

Wink didn't get a chance to answer because the monster slung a clump of wet tangled hair at the tiger, which at it's high speed would've shattered bones easily. Marble Proof didn't get time to be impressed at Wink's dodge because the hair clump jerked and around came at the rabbit. He shot up high and descended wielding his briar weapons. Without any words, the tiger and rabbit commenced to charging, jumping, slashing, biting, etc. at the behemoth.

The Uh On monster seemed quite a bit more agile than any other that Wink had fought. It dawned on the tiger as he scampered up the creatures back that if the Uh Oh had sworn off honey suckle glazed fried butter babies, no wonder he was so not-sluggish.

All to say, the rabbit and tiger made no progress towards a defeat of the creature and seemingly both realizing it at the same time, they both hit the ground and fled together.

"Sorry I wasn't much help" Marble Proof apologized mid-hop.

"No need to apologize" Wink returned mid-lunge. "This one's got the upper paw."

"Any ideas?"

The tiger seemed to shrug in spite of his sprinting. "I think what we're doing right now is the best idea."

But it wasn't the best idea, they soon discovered. The Uh

Oh monster was now chasing them and was much faster than them. It was only a matter of time.

"Any last thoughts?" the rabbit asked the tiger as they raced past the injured Thick Whisker Follow Feeders.

Wink laughed. "Yes — this is absolutely the last time I try to bail my cousin out of trouble."

"I think you'll get to tell this personally to his half-digested face in a few seconds."

The two were enjoying their last few seconds outside the guts of the monster when they ran up on the Oh Uh Activists, still wailing in their unmentionables.

"Get your telescopes out, guys" Wink said with a wicked grin the two sprinted past the clueless bunch.

And it was a little after this run-by that the rabbit and tiger noticed that the monster was no longer on their heals. In his next leap, Marble Proof spun around midair to take a look.

"Oh my!" the rabbit proclaimed landing to a stop.

The tiger slowed to join the looking and found himself watching the Uh Oh monster dinning happily on the activists.

"How can that be?" Marble Proof asked.

Wink shook his head. "Yeah, I don't get it either. Why not the feeders but yet people in their under...oh, I get it." The tiger started laughing.

The rabbit made a questioning noise.

Still laughing, Wink explained, "Well, I guess cause they look like big babies in their big diapers!"

Marble Proof didn't smile but in a rush of sympathy and opportunity, commanded while shooting up into the air, "Come on big kitty, let's seize our chance!"

And the two began again to fight the Uh Oh, who surprisingly held his own while munching on the activists. It was as if he weren't even trying.

Wink went to look for Marble Proof to express his opinion that this was still a losing battle but the rabbit was no where to be seen. The tiger's heart sunk a little, accepting that his new friend my must finally be dead.

But then an odd sight distracted him from his sorrow — one of the idiots appeared to have had a serious load in the back of his underwear. Wink couldn't help but chuckle at the sight of an adult who crapped themselves. But then caught himself, thinking about what Marble Proof would've said with his monk-mentored understanding of all people. Regardless how foolish, all folks deserved a chance to change their ways. And as it happened, the monster was leaning over to grab Activist Crap Pants.

So as a last tribute to the rabbit, Wink leapt towards the terrified human in an attempt at rescue. But as he went to grab the man, the loaf in the idiot's skivvies punched him in his good eye! The tiger fell away hurt and now blurry-blind.

When he finally got his good eye to begin working again, Wink looked to see the activist legs get slurped up into the Uh Oh's mouth.

"Sorry, hostile turd-cutting activist" the tiger said as empathetically as he could manage.

Wink decided this was a lost cause and trotted a safe distance away, deciding to at least study the Uh Oh's ways better, looking for movement patterns and composition weaknesses. Some helpful notes were made in the tiger's mind when all the sudden, the creature hesitated and began patting above it's belly, as if it had indigestion. Wink didn't get a chance to smile a serves-ya-right-you-got-indigestion smile because exactly where the monster was patting, blood, bone, flesh — and a briar numb-chuck wielding rabbit — gushed out in full force.

"Behold!" Marble Proof proclaimed in a gurgle of Uh Oh fluid. "Clinging turd, hidden rabbit technique, developed by Brother SeFlyn"

The tiger began laughing in joy and ran to join in wrapping up the battle against the Uh Oh monster.

Marble Proof and Wink stood together in the tiger's front yard, while SlipStep wandered around the yard, pretending to kung fu fight invisible menaces as best he could with his wooden prosthetic body.

"Thank you for taking him off my paws" the elder tiger said.

"No problem" the rabbit replied. "Well, that might not be true, but I'd like the challenge of sanding down your cousin's rough edges."

"That's putting it nicely."

"Promise you'll come visit the monastery soon. It'll do SlipStep good to have you see what he's accomplished."

"I wouldn't count your maggots until they've squirmed, bunny."

Marble Proof grinned but then raised an eyebrow watching Wink's one eye enlarge.

"Uh oh" the tiger quietly exclaimed.

The rabbit spun around to see a giant metal creature standing over the tiger's house and tightly grasping a screaming SlipStep in it's metal hands. And at the exact same time, both Wink and Marble Proof spied the tiny water pipe sticking out of the monster's head.

"Tell your abbott, I'm sorry I ever doubted him" the tiger uttered while bending down, readying a leaping stance.

"Understood" replied the rabbit pulling out a variety of burnt briar weapons.

At that, Wink and Marble Proof leapt into action against the water pipe.

Your Days Appeal to Me

If you're somewhere that you can see over the landscape of a forest, you might can sometimes spot teeny tiny hills that protrude out and over the tree tops. There's one in particular that I saw one day while squinting my eyes that had two benches and a path that ran over it.

And every so often when I see a woodsy path I take it, hoping it will spill me on to that particular teeny tiny hill. I haven't came across it yet but I did hear a story from a guy down at the Shady Tree Tea House bout two souls who did.

There was a baggy saggy eyed man who was using the path to get from one place to another. As he ascended the trail, he saw it was leading him to one of the benches on the teeny tiny hill. He sighed a sigh of welcome relief for he was plumb wore out and needed a good sit down.

And at the point in ascent when the sun shone on his head, the man spied the second bench with a girl sitting on it. She had marbles woven into hair and she was very pretty.

As he arrived at the bench he had designs on, the pretty

woman smiled at him, stood up and bowed, at which he took as permission to join her on the teeny tiny hill.

"Thank you for not protesting my presence", the baggy saggy eyed man said as soon as he got himself parked down on his bench.

"Thank you for not passing me by", the marbled hair girl said sweetly.

"Have you come here to rest?" the man asked.

"No, I never need anymore rest than I already get. I came here to have a look-see" the woman said letting her eyes glance over the tree top landscape.

The man followed her gaze and nodded yawning. "Well, I came to rest."

"What's wearin' ya out?" the woman with marbles in her hair asked, returning her gaze to the man.

The man inhaled and let out, "My days are pretty busy."

"How so?"

The man grimaced a little, not terribly enthused to relive his brand of bustle. But in an effort to sate the pretty girl, he slowly started to give some recitation.

"My days are always pursuits of difficult items to acquire.

It's how I put food on my table and am able to maintain the maintenance of those table legs when they falter. For example, today I ascended up Old Graveylady Mountain for an acquisition".

"Oh?" the woman asked with voice indicating she was craving more details.

The man shifted his legs on the bench to a settled comfortable entanglement and now seemed ready to rattle his teeth eloquently for the marbled hair woman.

"Now gettin' up that particular mountain requires me sweet talking a mid-mountain dweller into lending me one of their mountain billy snails in exchange for me making a craft out of sticks, tree sap and whatever I find in my pocket. Today I made a stick gum doll with a one-dull-toothed Gillyfish head.

"Then I ride the billy snail as far up Old Graveylady Mountain as it can go, tie it to a perturbing root and tell it that it even though it has a shell, it's not a fat creature (snails of all types have always been insecure bout this, mainly because slugs of all types is always mocking the 'wide load' creatures. Put your ear close to a snail and slug sticky cross trails and you will hear the echoes of bating and crying).

"From there, I climb up the rocks until I can climb no more and then pull out my iddy bitty lasso. When I spy a swarzagnat, which as you may know are bout as big as an eye grit, I rope it, secure the line, pull out another lasso and lie in wait for another. Even though they're incredibly strong, I still need to rope around 20 swarzagnats before I can get myself airborne and then in a short time, domesticate them so they won't slam me into the side of the mountain.

"Once all that gets goin', I steer them and myself to the side of a particular plateau called Ganderprop. There the hand-sized CronKaws mock the world below and how stupid they find it. These creatures are dangerously violent but fear death less than losing argumentative strongholds in their beliefs. This is why they rant from so high up and self mutilate their ears — they rarely have to hear a reply from those below.

So I wait in hiding until I see one finish a rant against everybody down below, extend a lewd hand gesture and then wander off from the others to relieve himself under a lo fi tree. You may know this but a lo fi tree photosynthesizes with sound and thus absorbs and deadens noises, particularly those frequencies under it. Most people do their business there to deaden the 'business' noises, which works out for me in that I can do what I need to do with the whizzin' CronKaw without his tribe hearing us.

"So under the lo fi tree, I confront the shocked urinator and counter something he said in his rant. CronKaws are creatures of feelings and reactions and so have little time for facts. Thus to a decent arguer who is careful not get trapped in their games of emotion can prove to them thoroughly they have no truth to back up their passionate beliefs. Today I did so by pointing out all his rant consisted of was claims to know the secret motives of people who disagreed with his beliefs. The CronKaw finished his 'business' and then shot back with the cliché cop out of 'My beliefs are conclusions of good will and thus those who oppose them are evil'. I returned with the historical point that pretty much every dictator and genocidal maniac had in their mind good intentions, thus the morality of will is at best relative, depending whether your viewing it from the throne or firing line. At which the CronKaw conceded defeat, though not verbally or intentionally. One can tell this by the fact the creature has laid an egg about ten times bigger that himself.

"So today as always at this point in my day, I grabbed the egg and ran for my life. The CronKaw chased me and screamed, at which his comrades became alerted and joined in pursuit. I sprinted around the plateau edge, quickly scanning below for clumps of fluffy white, which are Buffalug webs and are very soft and incredibly elastic. If I plan my leap just right, I land right in the middle of the webs which is as pleasant as falling into your bed at the end of a long day.

"The Buffalug is always a little alarmed at your dropping in and so today I apologized, asked for a cup of coffee and made small talk about things Buffalug are known to enjoy. Today we chatted about what annoying upstairs neighbors the CronKaws make.

"From here, I usually climb out of the web, slide some down the mountain and find the billy snail. I reward his patience with a bag of famous oppirg chips (saltless of course) and we slime on down back the mid-mountain point for rental returns and my own gratitudes to the mid-mountain dwellers.

"At this point, my egg and me usually travel south to the arid Isidro lands and climb a random high rock, scanning the horizon for children's birthday parties. It may take days but eventually you spy one. Today there was one that started up not a few minutes after I started lookin' and hopin'.

"So at that point, I come up on it and replace the birthday piñata with the egg, for only the blind swings of children can break open a CronKaw egg. The blindfolded kids bust open the egg, they scramble to grab all the jewels and valuable stones and I wait for the dust to clear to acquire a book wrapped in cahnny leaves.

"You see, CronKaws like to rewrite history to accommodate their theories and thus have to dispose of ancient books, scrolls or tablets that counter their untruthful side of the story. The also find cahnny leaves delicious and so mix fine dining and intellectual dishonesty for a rather delightful meal, I'm told.

"From there I take the ancient book to a monastery of the Salvage Shaolin order. There the junk monks will preserve and recopy the manuscript, make a little cash in sales to maintain their quiet lifestyle and they send me home with a nice gift basket, full of delicious food untainted by any recipe that fears death. They also include a pouch of royalties from the last book, scroll or tablet I pulled out of an egg for them.

"I've been doing pretty well cubbard-wise lately so today when I crossed paths with a Maker minister collecting food for Orphans of Insects Who Lost Their Parents to Magnifying Glasses, I gave him half the basket."

The tired eyed man started to add to the day's account about an odd incident that occurred after leaving the minister but felt it would confuse the flow of the tale. (I will tell you though — when the Maker preacher was out of earshot, the baggy saggy man's eye caught a teeny tiny Milly Cub surfing the breeze on a pink paper cut out heart. The tired man snatched the paper just to take a look, which seemed to frighten the milly and she jumped off and onto the ground.

He called out apologies and tried to offer it back it's pink flying machine but the milly cub called back in her jog, "I was almost to where I was headed; so keep the heart!"

The baggy saggy eyed man was sure there was some great story behind how the little cuddly creature came to be riding the cut out but in his line of work, it wasn't uncommon to be part of a story you didn't know the beginning or end to.)

So at his decision not to include the story, the man breathed a little outta breath from everything else he told and shrugged. "So, on a day like today, if I can get home before night fall I do, but a lot of times I end up sleeping in uncomfortable mega nightcrawler caves or wherever.

"But yeah, that's what one of my days might read like."

And with an attempted suppressed but undoubtedly electrified response, the marbles hair woman said, "Your days appeal to me".

The man shrug-smiled while considering this phrase and looked out over the leafy horizon. And then he turned towards her and asked, "Why did you come here to this teeny tiny hill to have a look-see?"

"I don't have too much to look at during my days."

"Hmmm…" the man replied, seemingly savoring the thought. "What's that like?"

"Well," the woman said crinkling her eyebrows, "nothing."

"It may seem like nothing but even silence and darkness are composed of something."

"Well, I guess my days are composed of 'something' if you consider waking up…", the woman looked her feet and thought, "…because your cat is pushing it's wet nose against your mouth and purring could be counted as 'something'."

"Go on" the man encouraged feeling more relaxed at the picture the marbled hair girl had begun painting.

She shrugged and continued. "Okay well...I wipe my face off, try to gather my morning senses and then I check under my pillow...", she reported looking away blushing some, "...for anything left underneath it. Ever since I was a child, someone has randomly left items under my pillow ranging from money to candy to seeds to odd rock dolls. I used to assume it was my dad but after he died, stuff kept ending up under there.

"Anyway, today I found a foreign coin commemorating The Great Brick Mis-Stack of '49AFA."

The baggy saggy eyed man laughed in wonderment.

"And then I check the cat's prosthetic legs and make sure it's spoons is still on good. It's utensil limbs gets loose sometimes in the night.

"From there, I pour my handicapped kitty it's cream, which is a recipe of sugar lilly dew and milk squeezed from the tiny yet perky bosom of a judybug."

The marbles hair woman seemed she was about to end the account but the baggy saggy eyed man encouraged her spirit with his verbal indications of listening pleasure of what she'd reported thus far. This made her smile and continue.

"At that point I pour myself some iced smiley face tea, put on an ugly sun hat and sit in my flower garden. The kinderflowers hum the one note they know and I harmonize or make up a melody around it.

"Then I scribble little lines of poems based on what I can remember from my dreams on the backs of jenelleybean wrappers and when a flying nut turtle flutters within reach, I tie the poemed papers to it's tail with a strand of my hair. It flies away and I watch it until I can't see it anymore.

"Then I imagine various scenarios of the notes getting found by somebody sad that might cheer up at reading them or a child getting excited at finding a wrapper only to be disappointed at it's absence of candy."

The bagged and sagged eyed man kept humming throughout the remainder of the girl's itinerary report, which included highlights of visiting some old men she called the Sewed Shut Eyed Shut-ins; digging holes in the backyard and taking anything crazy interesting she found in them (like shiny glob clusters, ancient lost socks, dirt worm bicycles, etc.) into town to sell to people who collect crazy interesting things; dusting her house, sweeping and dumping the debris into summer moth fields, and then watching the winged creatures roll around in the dirty clouds.

"There's variances in my day's activities," she concluded, "but they nearly always crescendo with a walk up here to these benches to watch the skyline, me praying for something exciting to look-see at."

The baggy saggy eyed man was chuckling still at certain elements of her delightful tale. And then he added, "Your days appeal to me".

Now this author still hasn't found a trail that leads to these benches but one day recently I did catch sight of the teeny tiny hill in my squinting. And I saw two figures sitting separately on those benches, one holding a basket, the other holding a paper heart and both seeming to be very much at peace. And after having to rub my eyes from all the strain the squinting does to 'em, their silhouettes had become figures holding hands.

A beam of sunlight made me blink and lose focus again. But when I relocated the teeny tiny hill on the leafy horizon, I only could see two empty benches. And though I don't know for a fact, I'm passionately hopeful that I had seen the very baggy saggy eyed man and the marbles hair woman on the teeny tiny hill.

Regardless of who I saw, two people were sharing their days together. And that gives this author hope.

Never Wanted, Never Noticed

There was a person thingy who had no home.

And so it went out looking for one to live in.

Sadly, Person Thingy always tried to enter the homes that didn't want it.

Or homes that had no room for it.

One home did allow Person Thingy to sleep under the foundation but it was full of snakes and grand daddy long legs.

Another took it in for a few days and it was the warmest few days of it's life. But then this home asked Person Thingy to leave to make room for a returning border.

And so Person Thingy walked under the hateful rain...

...every night slept under the cold skull in the sky.

Then it decided to enter homes that welcomed Person

Thingy but it really didn't want to enter. And inevitably Person Thingy would be kicked out for never sitting down.

Or sometimes it had to escape, for many of these homes were haunted or on fire.

And so the homeless Person Thingy decided to build it's own home.

It was a lonely dump but it kept Person Thingy dry and warm.

But on some days the wind carried the laughter and music from the other homes. This kept Person Thingy from sleep but also reminded it that it was not privy to happiness like everyone else.

Person Thingy tried building homes for it's ears but still heard the noise. It was so tired.

It was then that Person Thingy realized that both Brother Nature and other persons wanted it dead. It prayed but the Maker never seemed like He was going to intervene.

So Person Thingy made arrangements so that it was able sleep undisturbed for the rest of it's minutes.

And Brother Nature and the other persons rejoiced.

Or maybe they just never really noticed his existence or absence, either one.

Grumpskid

There was a woman that did many difficult things. Sometimes she ate fire cakes and then swallowed emotions so cold, they had became tangible ice chunks. Other times she forced freewill drunky monkeys to kiss her. And yet other times she told people what she didn't like about them, only to holler louder her praises of them when they protested. If you were lucky, she only sniffed fire hydrants after you leaked on 'em, just to put her big nose into your business.

But the bigger issue was that the woman often put into action her strong beliefs about how other people's lives should be ran. This ranged from some people waking up finding their house had been repaired in the night, to other people waking up to find their house riddled with electric fist holes. Sometimes the woman's convictions led her to cradle the heads of the hurting and at other times led her to black bruise the heads of those that she found to be morally slippery.

Not surprisingly, the woman — Compacist Grumps was her name — didn't have many friends and of the few she had, they often were reviewing the various available means of escape. I mean who could foretell when her caress was going to ball up into a fist.

One day after one of Ms. Grumps's friends refused to both change her hairstyle and go with her on a broken bone hunting trip (To explain this — Compacist would find people hobbling along with casts or splints, force them to painfully take off their mends and put on ones she had made for them. The new patch ups were often not as good as the ones removed but they at least had her name printed on them. And all this made Compacist Grumps feel accomplished, in spite of the screams and the whimpers of those she helped), the woman decided to go out by herself. Someone must've warned all the broked bone people cause there were nary a fracture in sight that day.

But after a spell of creeping and hunting, Compacist did catch a little crossed-eyed boy with a casted arm singing a happy song. The song particularly offended her, a bottom feeder glorification of a local historical legendary hot girl named Full Belly Fulcinda. So, the woman broke off the cast, re-mended it with a glob of swamp glue and industrial staples. Ms. Grumps then commanded the now whimpering boy pick back up with the happy song. This author can't tell if the boy was angry or in so much pain that he couldn't sing, but Compacist Grumps declared him ungrateful of her mending and pushed him into a glass tree, which of course shattered and gave the boy more to not sing about.

"He must learn to accept charity" Compacist Grumps said

to herself as she marched justifyingly away from the moaning, squirming bloody boy.

After some more woody walking, Ms. Grumps came into a field and right in the middle of it was a small hill or a giant pile, depending on one's perspective. Either way, it was made of poop. The summer sun was cooking it nicely and so to avoid the stench, Compacist Grumps started to head up another up windy direction. But a glimmer of something in the monster turd caught the woman's eye. From afar it looked like a jewel.

"Hmmm..." said Compacist Grumps, "I wonder what who made that loaf has been eating?"

In those parts it wasn't uncommon for Noswippy Dragons, Corner Toothed Mega Birds and other ginormous flying creatures to drop a load whilst cruising over. And if the monsters had been partaking in creative diets, whoever found the logs — and were adventurous enough to go digging — could really hit pay dirt. Just last week Kicky Guerra found a wash machine, an ant tusk and a human baby in a basket boat inside a steaming mound of what seemed to be cowcroaker droppings.

Compacist Grumps took a tug of what now appeared to actually be a chunk of metal buried in the dung. But in an attempt to not get her hands soiled, the woman couldn't really get a grip good enough to pull the item out of the thick fibrous manure (note — some peoples are known to actually make cloths, bricks and toys out of giant lumps of cowcroaker stool, given it's incredibly thready consistency. No one knows what possesses a person to do such a thing, although a social scholar at a city way far away named Dr. Glordia Chompy did study these "crap crafters" — as they're unaffectionately known — and the doc's report could only conclude that two traits linked them all: 1) They all had no sense of smell and 2) none were ever invited to sunset potlucks or moonlight dances. Even the dumbest drool duffis wearing a diaper on it's head could've reached those same conclusions and with far less of the tax payer's cash. But what also was found but not published in the report were the additional linking traits of crap crafters. Which were — 3) they always did everything their parents told them not to do and, 4) in village elections, they voted without fail for politicians whom commissioned worthless studies. This author only knows these hidden findings because of his brief romantic entanglement with a lab tech in Chompy's institute, whom told everything she knew after drinking too many fermented acorn slushys. The said author exited quickly from the tech's floppy lab coated arms as soon as he realized his own personal "findings" were being blabbed to whoever bought the moderately attractive tech an acorn slushy.)

All that said, Compacist Grumps eventually found some pupas nearby and convinced them that there was some delicious buttered cornycakes within the metal thingy. A half hour and 3 crap faced pupas later, Compacist Grumps had what was a strange metal box. And after dangling a large cuddle slug over a salt block and demanding it lick the box clean, the cranky woman was at home inspecting the mysterious although somewhat slug-sticky contraption.

The box was full of what looked to be formerly working lights, portals and frayed wires. Compacist Grumps thought after some light inspection that the gadgets could've been confused for an upside down face. This led her to turn the box upside down, which produced a right side face on a box.

"A robot head!" Compacist Grumps proclaimed with much joy.

Why this proclamation is a kicker, is when her elderly neighbor Edna Breakdown had bought a robot elbow at a rummage sale to replace her own arthritic elbow, Compacist Grumps had voiced aloud whenever she could how this body altercation was unnatural and was tampering with Brother Nature's intention for Ms. Breakdown to have a painfully bum elbow. Compacist Grumps was so strongly offended at both the prosthetic elbow and her neighbor's disregard for her opinions, she felt it justified her to send tiny party invitations to some micro metal munching meal worms. The worms showed up in their party dresses to the addy on the invites — Ms Breakdown's crib — and although found it hardly a happenin' party, did console themselves at the sight of the robot elbow and proceeded to eat through it as if were a crispy fried jelly pie to you or I.

But as is often the case, it's easy to be morally opposed to a convenience that one does not actually have access to. So in a quick turnaround, Compacist Grumps became an avid robotics enthusiast and started to investigate on how to get the big metal head working again.

The grumpy woman started running through her mind all the mechanically minded souls in and around her village. There was Shelwee the lurky turkey farmer who had built robot street lamps for the village (the lamps patrolled their assigned streets and walked alongside anyone traveling until meeting another lamp, at which the illuminating bots fist bumped and exchanged escortees. This author's favorite lamp bot feature was how they could hike up their legs at the sight of oncoming dogs, if ya know what I mean).

But Compacist Grumps had burned her bridges with Shelwee after the farmer had enlisted her lurky turkeys in the great war with the Puddle Sniffers (her birds would lurk around the enemy encampments, eavesdropping and then run back, gobble gobbling all the intel they had gleaned). Opposed to the war that didn't actually directly involve their village, Compacist Grumps felt it was her duty to stunt the flow of information and so carried with her at all times a salt shaker, a bottle of spicy cream sauce and bread so when/if she bumped into one the sneaky turkeys, she prepared it for digestion and ate it thus. Although every bird made the woman sleepy afterwards, one fat one in particular whom she found out later was taking cold medicine, caused her to completely pass out during the last couple of swallers. The farmer found Compacist Grumps fast asleep with lurky bones all around and swore never to forgive the woman for her treason.

Then there was D Dawg Tarps, who engineered robotic edible self buttering popcorn for the local dirt puppet theater. But there was a burned bridge there too. It's a story that I best not mention involving D Dawg, Compacist in a well-ventilated blouse, a starry night and buttery fingers.

The only other potential aid Ms Grumps could think of was Rosemander, who didn't know diddly bout robots but had a cousin in another village who had dated a guy who did. The cousin reportedly caught the guy in an well ventilated scenario involving one of his robots, a starry night and buttery fingers and so ditched the guy but kept all his robots and now runs a robot wonderland for less fortunate nine-fingered kids.

So Compacist Grumps stuffed the head in a bed grit bag, moseyed on over to Rosemander's home where the latter was outside playing her all-weather limestone piano in the garden. The piano playin' girl smiled hesitantly when she saw the woman walk up. Compacist Grumps raised up a ninja's triple buzz action sledge saw over the piano and presented Rosemander with options.

After a phone call was put into her cousin, Rosemander applied her new knowledge to Compacist's robot head and after a little wire and circuit fiddling, the head hummed to life. The ninja sledge saw holdin' woman grabbed the contraption from the piano player, threw the bag over it and hurried back home.

Once in the dark privacy of her home, Compacist Grumps

uncovered the robot head, which from it's mechanical eyes seemed to be trying to get it's bearings.

"What's up?" the head greeted.

Compacist Grumps wasn't quite prepared for conversation and so fumbled, "Um, nothing, — well except you, I suppose."

"Thanks for that" the head said. "Waking me, I mean."

"Not a problem. Well, I can't say that it wasn't some problem but it's sewage under the bridge now. How was it that I found you in a giant pile of excrement, or do you not know?"

The head's gears whirled a little. "Let's see — the last thing I remember was...uh...oh, yes, now I can follow those events to the excrement."

Compacist Grumps was getting a little impatient. "Which were...?"

"Well, my last memory was of being chewed on by a large reptile. So I'm guessin' I must've been swallowed, where after I rode the intestinal train to where you found me. Sounds probable. Unless of course the reptile was eaten by an even bigger beast, at which I might've ridden shotgun in that creature's digestive express-"

"Yes, yes — I get all the possible variables involving you

and monster waste caves! But how was it you were being eaten by a giant anything in the first place?"

"Well by orders of my owner Mr. Westayaycon, I was attacking a city that did not appreciate his silky smooth vocal stylings enough to give him a pin-on medal."

"Oh" Compacist Grumps nodded. "That must've been Beanstween Dabread Town. I heard about that incident and do you know they still don't know who the perpetrator was?"

"That's interesting" the robot head commented. "So anyway, since you're now my current owner, let me know what you need destroyin' and I'll get crackin'."

Compacist Grumps was silent for a spell but feigned an appalled faced. "No sir! I'm a woman of peace! There'll be no destruction via your robotics on my watch!"

The head considered this with some circuit hums and then quickly conformed. "As you wish. My metallic casing is strong enough to crack nuts with and I also make an excellent night light."

Compacist Grumps nodded. "Well, that's more like it. Welcome to your new home and regardless of what you were called before, you're getting a new name to symbolize a change for the better. You shall be known as...er...HumHead!"

And so Compacist Grumps and HumHead became an inseparable item of sorts. In addition to the skills the robot head had already highlighted, Ms. Grumps found him also useful as a music box, spell checker and — by way of his laser beam eyes — a bread toaster! Although the grumpy lady would've opposed it had she known, HumHead also used his lasers to blast bump baker bugs and dysenterytown microbes while she relaxed in her outdoor fennel bubble baths. Subconsciously Compacist Grumps might've detected the change in the pest population because she once stated openly to her metal friend that she'd never been this relaxed while naked in all her life.

And that said, her village which had not been that relaxed in sometime, sighed easy for those few glorious weeks. There were even popular butt jiggling tunes written in commemoration of Compacist Grumps' current preoccupation, keeping her home and away from meddling in people's daily affairs.

One of the few friends of Compacist I mentioned earlier — named Jellychin Judes — also noticed a pleasant change in her friend's disposition and began to visit the woman voluntarily. Jellychin was suspicious of Compacist Grumps's change of heart but eventually accepted without any explanation the sudden turnaround.

One day while the two ladies were playing the game of idabird bones — HumHead playing exotic salsa music of the ice swamp regions of Limaltmitlands — the older woman asked with an inquisitive smile, "So Jellychin — how's your heart and is anyone sniffing around it?"

Jellychin shook her head. "Compacist, you put that like a pack of stray boys are bout to lick my heart or urinate on it, one."

"They all will if you let them. One got butter and salt all over my heart, ya know."

"Not all boys are as slippy fingered as D Dawg Tarps. But in answer to your question, there is one fella that I've been lettin' peek over my fence."

"Name?" Compacist Grumps asked grinning delicious as she threw two idabird bones in the game thimble.

"Massey Massey the Roof Sweeper" Jellychin reported unable to keep up feigning indifference, her face swept into a beaming smile.

Compacist Grumps had went to shake the bone bowl, paused and after a slight inhalation, continued the game.

Jellychin continued. "I know you may not approve, but — and no offense — you never do."

Ms. Grumps miraculously kept her grace. "Jellychin, I'm sure he's okay. I just never liked his sister."

Jellychin swallered, vaguely remembering some rumors of

an altercation tween her grumpy friend and the sweeper's sister.

"So back to the matter at hand," Compacist went on, "have you two had your first stroll neath the glass branches?"

And Jellychin, with initially some guardedness, let out some of the vague details of she and Massey Massey's flirtings. But soon Jellychin in a great desire to proclaim her happiness aloud, trusted the new Compacist Grumps and in the course of the Idabird game dished out all the warm details. The women smiled and chatted all through the night to the glow and salsa of the robohead.

Now a month or so passed without anything of interest transpiring in and around the village. But a little after this span of calm, something odd did go down. Jellychin was walking down Grasstain Street (side note — if ever you find yourself on this particular stretch, you really should pop into Drunk As A Genetically Predisposed Skunk On A Predestined Monk for a jar of their house sauce. It's terrible on it's own but is stellar with a side of ditch litter jerky!) and came across a commotion at the skirt tailor's shop. There were village volunteer stewards, onlookers and such gathered outside the shop. To no one in particular Jellychin posed, "Que pasa?"

A random voice Jellychin never did focus on answered, "There's been a big robbery! Some one got off with a lot of skirts!"

"Well, the next woman we see tryna wear 15 skirts at once, is soooo busted!" said another.

There were a few laughs at the absurd scenario until someone countered as if the latter comment had been serious, "This may've not been a crime of fashion! The skirt tailor had a lot of enemies that would love to see him destitute!"

The lingering laughing ceased and many in the crowd agreed with their moans and head nods.

"Yep, when you meddle in people's lives, you gotta expect a little meddling in return!" someone agreed.

"What some call 'meddling', others call 'courage'!" another person added.

Some in the crowd clapped and some booed in disagreement.

The skirt maker's meddling/courageousness
was his watchful eye over couples in the village expecting children. If at around the time of birth the couples were seen with no children or expectations, the tailor quietly was on the case. It saddens this author to report but in this and many villages in the region, some parents secretly disposed of children that didn't come out as hoped. Bum limbs, deformed heads, wrong eye color, too many chins, grating coos, not a clear vision for the future and sometimes just bad timing. Truth be told, some of the unwanted babies

weren't even babies and in some cases were a few miles down the adolescent road when their parents fired them.

Either way, the preferred method of "letting them go" was putting them in baskets with little sails during extremely breezy nights and leaving their fates to the winds. Some babies actually fared well after being found in other towns, revered by the finders as blessed or incredibly lucky, and a sense of destiny filling the hearts of those families that took in the "wind orphans".

But sadly most children died from any amount of the danger an infant can fare blowing around in the sky. As one who was a wind orphan himself, I can tell ya my sextuplet siblings went several ways back to the Maker. Impalement by telerphone pole, inhalation by a cloud custodian's vacuum cleaner, mastication by a flying cowcroaker and suffocation after being swept under a tundra rug. One of my sisters was used by a night ghoul to plug a hole in the sky. I don't know what happened to her beyond this but I can't imagine it were good.

So long ago in his travels to find materials for his skirts, the tailor had come across one too many remains of dead babies and so took it upon himself to save as many as he could. When the terrible parents laid the children out in the wind basket boats, the skirt weaver snatched them up, found them welcome homes and in some cases kept a few for himself. With the latter he always snuck away from the place of abandonments whispering to these children that looked at him with the "keep me!" doe eyes the lyrics of a popular song, "Mama, ya sure ya don't want this smile sweet?/ never no mind — that leaves more for me!"

You can imagine the conflict of the emotions some townspeople had when going to buy a skirt and being waited on by a child that they had thrown away. Some of the fickle parents were secretly grateful to the tailor while others let their guilt turn into despisement of the meddler.

All to say, the skirt weaver had indeed earned a few enemies.

"Maybe it was one of his bratty slave kids?" someone in the crowd cackled.

Some folks 'amened' and others hissed at whoever made the cynical quip.

Jellychin, a bit of a fan of crime scenes, studied the outside of the shop for clues that maybe the village stewards might've missed. But with nothing much out of place or visually broken — doors and windows completely intact — Jellychin decided to just give the shop owner and his children her sympathies and her pledge to buy more skirts in the upcoming months. The skirt kids hugged her, the tailor thanked her and Jellychin went on her way to have an appointed acorn coffee date with Massey Massey.

The next time Jellychin was over at Compacist Grumps's for a game of Skip My Turn Before I Lose This Stupid

Game, she brought up the robbery. He friend had continued to be withdrawn from village life and had not heard about the incident. Jellychin told the woman what she knew, which wasn't much more than what you know, after which Compacist Grumps reacted with a shrug and told HeadHum to turn up his music volume a little.

"Let me get you a tissue" Jellychin reacted sarcastically.

"I don't know what you want me to say, Jellychin" the woman countered irritated. "Part of me doesn't care and the other part thinks the skirt maker had it coming, with all his meddling with Brother Nature's intent. But I can tell you the 'doesn't care' part is making the 'had it coming' part it's jail house girlfriend."

"Brother Nature's intent?" Jellychin asked stunned.

"The parents that gave up their kids were doing so because their brains told them too. You wait and see that the most of the 'breezy kids' or whatever they call them will grow up to be sickly or serial killers or societal leeches. Brother Nature put that impulse in the parent's brains for a reason.

"But again, I really don't care."

Jellychin remembered the old Compacist Grumps and realized that maybe things hadn't quite changed as much as she had thought. Although she didn't appear to act on them anymore, the woman still had a lot of the twitch-eyed convictions.

Jellychin dropped the subject and tried to finish the game without any more talk of found babies or stolen skirts.

On a stroll thru the Tealmont high grasses, known for their exquisite plastic pink flamingos hidden within, Massey Massey could tell something was eating at Jellychin. He asked and she told of her being bothered by Compacist Grumps's reaction to the skirt robbery.

"If I can speak freely..." the sweeper asked.

"You may" Jellychin granted.

"I know it bothers us when people we love can believe so differently than us or that some of our friends would certainly be on the opposing side if certain ideological wars broke out, but at least with Compacist, she just thinks things anymore, and that's it. I'd just be thankful that she no longer goes around sawing giggle giraffes legs down so the stumpy gargle giraffes won't get jealous. Or be glad she doesn't pee on old men with floppy hats like she used to for whatever conviction I never did catch, cause you know your grandpa would've qualified for a Compacist Grumps spray at the end of this year."

Jellychin smiled finally and took the roof sweeper's encouragement to let it all go. At this she let her head rest against Massey Massey's arm.

"Hey, I have something for you" her special fella announced.

"Really?" Jellychin asked looking up.

"Yes ma'am!" and at that her fella pulled out a metal sculptured chest plate with glass windows showcasing various images important to the girl, all with a key hole right in the middle of it.

"Oh my goodness!" Jellychin exclaimed. "I love it!"

"Thanks, though I can't take complete credit for it. I found it already a melted metal glob with a keyhole in it and just helped it with a little forging to look more like a heart and of course I added the bling around the hole."

"What's the bling made out of of? I never seen such a bright stone!"

"Well, since I found it on one the moonbeams I was sweepin' the other night, I decided to make it out of all chipped moonbeams I've been collecting over the years."

"Moonbeams?" she asked looking up and searching the boy's face for some punch line. "Are just tryna be poetic?"

Massey Massey cleared his voice a little and then in a whisper revealed, *"Actually, I am a moonbeam sweeper as well as a roof one! It's an old trade secret but I can tell you that in very bright nights, the older beams can be walked upon, while the younger you can slide down with great speeds.*

"Either way, they get dusty and need a good clean or else the moonlit nights would be dull, dark and stale."

"Are you messin' with me?"

"If I'm lyin' I'm dyin'! I'll take you on a night walk soon, where which we'll stroll upon the old bone's lights instead of just under it."

Jellychin studied the sweeper's eyes and after finding them void of falsehoods, believed him. And from this moment on, she never questioned his words ever again.

"Awww...you're great!" Jellychin cooed while resting her head on Massey Massey's arm again. Then suddenly looking up at the boy asked, "Hey — ya wanna make out?"

A few weeks later, another disruptive event occurred. The Theand family — who lived far out in the Motstiaw plains — had their grain silo punctured, letting all the fruits of their labors spill out. And by the time they found the mess, negra noches birds had carried off a majority of it in their plumage knapsacks. Many in the town, including Jellychin and Massey Massey, brought covered dishes and condolences to the family. Jellychin of course, went to the crime scene and studied the melted hole in the silo but could find no other clue to a motive or what the perpetrator might be. That is, except a printed-on-nice-cardstock party invitation that one of the Theand boys showed Jellychin. It read:

"Partaaaay 2nite! Get your glutton on at the Theand farm! Fully catered and dj provided. Just bring yoself, yo appetite and your knapsack!"

Jellychin excused her self and ran off to the Wispy Nest apartment mounds where the negra noches birds lived. When one bird went flying out of the mound for whatever reason, the girl nailed it in the belly with a marble shot via her semiautomatic sling shot. The bird tumbled to the ground, where Jellychin stood over it, another marble in the sling and demanded, "You — bird! Tell me bout the party tonight!"

Dazed and in pain, the bird spit out, "You effin' shot me!"

"You'll live — that is unlessin' you don't tell me what I need to know!"

"What's there to tell? We all got invitations in our mail boxes yesterday and so we went, had an effin' great time and took home enough leftovers to last us till the great Head Negra Noche Bird In Charge comes back and leads us into the Great Battle to peck all the human and cat eyes out!"

"That's it? Wasn't there a party host, a bouncer or any body else?" Jellychin questioned pulling the sling back harder.

"No, lady! Just us! I mean there wasn't even a dj like the invitation promised!"

"Hmmm..." Jellychin muttered while thinking to herself about this information or lack thereof.

"Can you put that thing down now?" the nervous bird pleaded more annoyed now that his senses were returning.

"Fair enough" Jellychin agreed lowering her weapon. "You're free to go but while I have you, tell your buddies to quit eating my Lady-Be-Good Bugs."

"What's your address?" the negra noches bird asked brushing his feathers off.

"Nice try. Just have your comrades quit eating any of them."

"I don't have that kind of pull — those insects are delicious!"

"Fine. Just pretend you had a vision that the Large And In Charge bird told you a great badness would come to ya'll if you keep eating any Lady-Be-Good Bugs."

"That's blasphemy!"

"Dude! Do ya know how many girlie birds will flutter around you when you end up predicting the future and looking like a prophet?"

"Do you know how many meals I'll miss when they excommunicate me?"

"The choice is yours."

"Somehow I think the choice has been taken outta my wings" the bird complained.

Jellychin shrugged, shot the negra noche bird mildly with one more marble and ran off into the night.

As the weeks went on, more and more bad incidents occurred, some mysterious and possibly random while others were clearly part of the same deliberate plot to cause misery upon particular people. Jellychin followed them all, made investigations and inquiries, but couldn't put enough pieces together to find a pattern or clear motive.

One of these particular peoples who suffered from the orchestrated tragedies I failed to mention was Massey Massey's sister ReneeHey. Someone tried to run over her with a space tractor, but luckily missed and only nicked her in the hip.

Jellychin reflected on all of tragic incidents with Compacist Grumps one early evening as the two strolled down Stubby Shrub Way, HumHead on hand to act as a lantern when the dark descended. Ms. Grumps listened to her inquisitive friend but didn't feign too much interest otherwise. Jellychin picked up on this and like before said so.

"I gotta say Compacist, for someone who in the past had her finger in about every other person's pie in and around the village, I can't get over how indifferent you are."

"I'm sorry if this makes me a bad friend but I'm still truly not interested" Compacist Grumps shrugged. "And even if I were, every single person that you mentioned that illness has fallen upon, I have completely no sympathy for. The Anoroc Twins are shallow, obnoxious drunks whom deserve that their boyfriends' exploded into dandelion helicopters! Fraazelbembap is a perpetual child who will wake up one day and wonder why no one cared enough to spank her. The Theand family are selfish weirdoes who only grow food for themselves and keep their kids from being 'tainted by common children' by keeping them on the farm. I remember asking Mr. Theand to donate some curly grain to a food drive I was organizing for the Puddle Sniffers and he slammed the door in my face!"

Compacist Grumps sighed before she added the next part of her tirade but continued unflinchingly all the same. "And do you know how many women ReneeHey makes feel inadequate, like they're less than real women, by her not hiding her apparent lack of time ravaged beauty? Of course you don't because you're blindly in love with her brother!

"So in conclusion, although I couldn't care less if you told me the village was attacked by a swarm of brain eating flying dustcrobes, if it did, I couldn't say most of those drooling sheep didn't have it coming."

Strangely, in spite of Compacist Grumps's venomous spew, Jellychin's attention had turned to something else: several times during the speech, the girl witnessed the robot head fry insects with it's laser beam eyes. Compacist Grumps never seemed to notice or care but what really struck Jellychin, was that one of the insects had obviously been in an accident and was thus fitted in a flying wheelchair. And when it flew too close to Compacist Grumps, HumHead both fried the bug and melted the wheelchair. That latter action put a shooting chill through her being.

Jellychin let a floating stream of cloud stuff caress her face as her hand repeatedly ran itself against the moon beam she and Massey Massey were sitting together on.

"I guess you're used to this," Jellychin said to her fella, "but I can't get over the texture and air of things up here."

Massey Massey shrugged. "I wouldn't say I take it for granted but sometimes there's so much to sweep, I have to leave the awe for another night."

Jellychin smiled letting her eyes shut but then remembering why they were there perched in the clouds. She took a look through the hole in the clouds that the sweeper had cut for her, down at Compacist Grumps's home and saw no change in the flickering winder lights and generally contained no notable indoor activity. This had been the fourth night in a row that Jellychin and her sweepin' fella had sat up here monitoring her toxic friend's house for some kind of clue to the great sad events of recent weeks.

"I hope I'm wrong about Compacist" Jellychin sighed, "but I can't help not ignore all the fingers pointing at her obvious motives."

"It must be terrible to suspect a friend of such horrible things" Massey Massey sympathized out loud.

"Yeah," Jellychin nodded almost ashamed of herself, "I remember some teenaged boy trying to tell me once that Compacist was a horrible person. He claimed she held him down behind the Skunk Drunk once, spray painted the words 'barn door of untruth' on his face along with an arrow pointing towards his mouth. He said he had to hide his face for weeks until the paint fell off with old skin. I thought it sounded like something Compacist would fantasize about doing but too hurtful for a person of her sometimes compassion to follow through with. I just thought some other thugs were getting creative about a generally unpleasant loud mouth.

"Now here I am — maybe about a couple months and three buckets of tears too late."

Massey Massey mused aloud, "I wonder when did Hitsain the Butcher's friends realize he'd crossed over from 'ambitious societal architect' to 'genocidal maniac'?"

"About 10 million dead Jurgs into it I believe is when they

switched his toothpaste to spinal cord liquifying poison ooze."

The sweeper nodded.

Jellychin looked away from Compacist Grumps's roof top to look sincerely in her fella's eyes. "I'm sorry I've drug you into all this drama. And I know you were hoping our initial time on the moonbeams would be special and romantic, not that spying on friends doesn't have a amorous element to it."

They both giggled a little at this.

"And," she continued glancin' up at the beam makin' moon, "I know the skull in the sky is a reminder of all things gone wrong, but I still would like to revisit it one day if you'd take me."

Massey Massey nodded. "It's quite a walk but, absolutely."

Jellychin smiled at her fella and added, "In spite of everything that's got our attention this moment, it doesn't mean while we're waitin' that...we...can't...", and then — well the two did their making out thing again.

They didn't get to do it for long because the blare of the village's Sorrow Horn broke all peace in the land and air.

"Oh no!" Jellychin exclaimed as she shot a look at her friend's house, which still sat there without much stirring.

There was some movement though, directly below the cloud Jellychin and Massey Massey hid in and the two leapt and let themselves slide down one of the young unweathered beams. Once down, they were surrounded by a gaggle of lurky turkeys.

"Did she get past us?" Jellychin asked fearing somewhere in their cloud chats, Ms. Grumps had snuck out.

The bird and former war hero known as Huhizs reported, "Gobble bobble sobble!" which translates as, "Naw, the old bag is still in there whispering sweet nothings to her toolbox!"

"For sure?" Jellychin pressed.

"Gobble tobble lobble!" Huhizs confirmed as his war medals jingled on his feathery chest.

Jellychin was slightly relieved that Compacist Grumps was absolved but still bothered by the perpetrator's identity still being unknown.

"Gobble fobble nobble!" reported another turkey running up to those gathered there.

"You saw a child running from this vicinity?" Jellychin clarified.

The lurky turkey nodded.

"Didja see where it ran off too?" Massey Massey asked.

The lurky turkey pointed with a sling of his wattle.

"Let's go!" and off up the closest old moon beam the sweeper jumped on to, Jellychin and Huhizs close behind.

Jumping from beam to beam, it didn't take long for Massey Massey to catch sight of the fleeing child from up in the night sky. Jellychin and the turkeys had a more difficult time keeping up, at times landing on a new slick beam and sliding down it before leaping to an old sustainable incline.

The sweeper finally found himself just a little ahead of the incredibly fast child and hit a young beam, sliding down at lightening speed, catching a bit of the child's hair before his feet hit the ground. The child slipped twisted around, Massey Massey now finding himself face to face with the kid, promptly followed by a punch to his own face.

As he fell backwards, he heard an apology before he hit the ground.

"Oh, it's you Mr. Massey" the child said. "I thought you were the monster or a noche negra bird, one."

The sweeper recovered from the punt and recognized one of skirt maker's wind orphans. Jellychin and Huhizs finally caught up and fell out of the sky, the turkey's beard a little outta place from the fall.

"Krisret, what were you doing outside Compacist Grumps's house?" Jellychin demanded.

The girl got a good look at the woman and the bird with her one good eye before answering with a, "I was watching her. My siblings and I suspect her of the robbery and the other trouble in town."

"Does you papa know you're out here right now?" Jellychin asked a little suspiciously.

"No ma'am. He's been so exhausted working double shifts to replenish everything that was stolen from us, he never hears us come and go. There's a thin line tween sustaination and starvation for a skirt tailor."

"Are your siblings out here too?"

"Somewhere, yes. We've been posting ourselves all about the surrounding areas in case Ms. Grumps's not the culprit."

"Any leads then?"

"Not yet. We can't help but see connections tween the bad things and Compacist Grumps's typical behavior but nothing we've seen can back our suspicions up. My theory is that she's puppeteering some minion to do her deeds, via a spell or some kind of guilt trip, one."

"I wonder if your other siblings saw whatever the Sorrow Horn was declaring."

"No. Tessa called me on my peanut phone, saying she was very near the area but only heard a commotion and somehow got her hair singed real good. Nothing else."

Jellychin sighed and after a few other questions, Krisret went on home leaving the two and their turkeys to themselves.

"What now?" Massey Massey asked.

His friend shook her head, discouraged. "I guess just study and sleep on it.

"Will you walk me home?"

And the sweeper obliged his girl but said nothing more, letting the girl do her private pondering in the cool night air.

The incident that occurred that night while Jellychin and her crew were monitoring Compacist Grumps's home was the destruction of a particular Esob plant station that broadcasted from the village. The music spun at the station broadcasted to all Esob teeny tinys throughout the region (the music bumped out it's leafy cones) and specialized in the Jumpy Accordion genre. Apparently the perpetrator was not a fan. But before burning the plant station to the ground, this destructive monster took over the broadcast and played a set of music that it liked, which was of the Authoritarian Folk genre. With phony baloney dumbed down 2 chord structures, the music carried the message of rich know-it-alls who painted their need for absolute power with lyrical imagery featuring missing flowers, changing the diaper of time and the safety felt in their barbed wire embraces.

The station program director, Cratedigger Dryfinger, was quoted later as saying she didn't know what was worse — the destruction of the station or the monster's set list.

Though the village had no laws and thus no law enforcement per se, there was an agreed upon mechanism that when someone or some event threatened the survival of the people or enough outcry was heard, the volunteer village stewards would come together to figure out what to do about it. And after the Esob plant occurrence, the outcry became overwhelming.

The stewards called everyone to the revival shelter the next day and let everyone have their say, giving their theories and proposals. Long story short — all fingers, including some broken ones, pointed at Compacist Grumps. There was miles of testimony, exhibitions of scars and accounts of the past nasty words spewed out of the woman's mouth.

(In must be noted that there were a few souls who although kept shy of defending the woman's general existence, did mention some of her positive moments. Most of those occurrences still ended up with results worse than when she got involved, but her good intentions were at least recognized.)

Right before the stewards began to open discussions as to what method of disposal of Ms. Grumps would be best, one last witness stood forward.

"I know that my friend Compacist Grumps is without a doubt a woman with a misguided heart" Jellychin Judes accounted. "We should've stood up to her a long time ago. But we're a village that's known as slow to judge and even slower to act. I'm proud of what we are, especially if you've visited other towns and cities where they quarantine every sneezer and ban suspicious twitches in their obsessive fear of any hint of anything out of the ordinary. Their citizens are haggard and live in fear of the city managers, which in many people's minds have become the great evil they all worked so hard to insulate themselves from.

"That said, I still feel that all the horrible incidents that have occurred recently — although they have the scent of Compacist Grumps — cannot be proven to be the acts of the woman. All the evidence we have is instinctive and circumstantial. We could be totally right but I feel a trial or an inquisition of Compacist is in order before a disposal is put forth. I ask that we err on the side of caution, because if a precedent is set on disposing of folks on just suspicions, we'll end up like those jerk towns we all drive around to avoid getting caught in."

Some in the revival shelter 'amened', while some grumbled their weariness of sitting on their hands. The village stewards, anxious to put off any kind of hard action, quickly decided amongst themselves to have Compacist Grumps brought to the shelter that evening.

While waiting for the retrievers to return with Compacist Grumps, Jellychin and Massey Massey bumped into the Skirt Maker and all his children.
"How are things, Mr. Skirt?" Jellychin asked, nodding at the smiling Krisret.

The father shrugged. "They're okay. It'll be spell before the business recovers but we're thankful for each other and making the best of things. And I'll feel better if they close the case on all this."

They all nodded and Jellychin smiled noticing Tessa's hair was shortened on one side.

"Hey," the skirt tailor exclaimed, "where did you get that chest plate, Ms Judes?"

"It was a gift from me", the sweeper jumped in. "I found the melted metal piece one night and did all the etchings and ornaments myself."

"Do you like it?" Jellychin asked.

"Well, yeah," the skirt maker answered rubbing the back of

his head, "particularly when it used to be the lock to my shop!"

Jellychin and Massey Massey were stunned but before they got a chance to establish that they didn't rob his shop, the tailor injected, "I even still have the key in my pocket! But really, it didn't look that good when I owned it. Hunh — who knows? Massey Massey, your talents are wasted on people's roofs! When I get past all my money troubles, I'm gonna commission you to...."

The skirt maker was interrupted by the commotion of a couple hefty women struggling to pull Compacist Grumps into the shelter. The heavies had singed hair and burn marks from HumHead's attempt at defending his owner but he was now frozen in a big ice cube, rendering him useless.

The inquisition was uncomfortable for all involved. Compacist Grumps's victims had to relive seeing the woman that had caused so much misery in their lives. And folks who hadn't felt the woman's wrath got to witness it that evening as she screamed at everyone, cursed them for whatever she felt their flaws were.

"YOU PEOPLE ARE PATHETIC AND DESERVE EVERYTHING AWFUL THAT BEFALLS YOU!", the furious woman howled. "IT'S JUSTICE FOR YEARS OF DOING THINGS THE WRONG WAY! THE SELFISH WAY! THE MEAN SPIRITED WAY! YOU'RE NOT REAL PEOPLE ANYMORE, JUST

DEFORMED DEFIANT BRATS WHO SPIT IN THE EYE OF BROTHER NATURE AND ANYBODY WHO TRIES TO HELP YOU! YOU THINK I'M THE ENEMY BUT I WAS ON YOUR SIDE! I DID SO MUCH FOR YOU PEOPLE. I WORKED HARD AND SACRIFICED SO THINGS COULD BE BETTER FOR THIS VILLAGE! AND THIS IS HOW YOU THANK ME! YOU'RE NOT WORTH THE OLD SPIT THAT DRIPS FROM THE NIPPLE OF..." But really you get the gist of Ms. Grumps's rant.

Jellychin felt that even though her friend proudly confirmed many of the accusations leveled against her and even bragged about many incidents unknown to the villagers up to that point, that the fact that she denied having any hand in the recent occurrences still might've meant that something or someone else was afoot.

In spite of all that, the final convicting finger was another hefty women's hauling in of a wheelbarrow of items soiled with mud and such. The hauler held up a few of the dirty things, which after a squint glance past all the filth one could spot prosthetic legs, fried pudding pies, melted accordions and many many skirts. These, the hefty woman revealed, were found buried in a mound a fat dog's toss from Compacist Grumps's home.

The village stewards in the end announced, that even if Compacist Grumps had nothing to do with all the recent crimes and the mound was some sort of attempted frame up, she had admitted to enough other offenses to garner some kind of action.

But before they could vocalize their plan of disposing of the woman, a tiny creature riding what looked like a paper plane with blackened wings sailed into the revival house and landed it's flying contraption on the shelter's pulpit.

After catching it's breath, the little being that in some parts is known as a Milly Cub, announced, "Dear people of whatever village I'm in right now — I was sailing through your town for reasons irrelevant to my chief message to you, which is that I arrived in the middle of a terrible incident in progress not minutes ago! I was sailing through a field full of grass and plastic flamingos when I came across a creature beating a buttery handed man with one of the beautiful pink statues!

"And so I flew into the creature and clawed at whatever I could. I didn't get much outside of ripping a chunk of it off before my chosen mode of transportation got burnt a bit by it's laser beam box. But I believe my impotent attack was enough at least to scare the thing off. I chased it onto the far side of the field and into an paella cuarto, where I employed some sneaky turkeys nearby to keep the creature pinned in the cooking house, where I hope it's still there as we stand here now.

"I must go now for reasons irrelevant to your monster problem but good luck to you and your village. Sincerely, me!"

And the Milly Cub kicked up his paper bird and flapped away, letting the supposed chunk of the monster flutter to the ground. One of the village stewards retrieved the item, and shook his head perplexed as he held up what was just a crinkly piece of paper that read the single word, "*not*".

Jellychin didn't stick around to hear the debate about letting a flying weird bear delay Compacist Grumps's fate. With the sweeper, the skirt maker's family and few others close behind, Jellychin raced off to the Tealmont grass field.

The scene at Fosty's Left Handed paella cuarto (an old legendary cookhouse where it was said a sprite had cooked meals that swayed a volcano to stop spewing it's volcanic fiery spittle onto the immediate land. The volcano is now known as Old Gravylady mountain.) was that of every few moments a fist of swirling letters jetting out of a window or hole, at which several of the lurky turkeys pecked away with their beaks until the script thing pulled itself back in. Whatever the creature was, it was screaming with language that sounded nearly coherent, though possibly backwards or with many of the key vowels removed. The birds were relentless, in spite of the fact that several of their comrades had been snatched by the beast, their licked bones tossed back out the windows after several good munchings.

This went on a for a spell while more and more villagers gathered round, including the bound Compacist Grumps and her guards. The stewards huddled together trying to make a decision, which is pretty difficult when one doesn't make decisions very often, especially where so many folks are affected.

While they debated amongst themselves, Huhizs strutted up with a piece of soft paper in his beak and handed it to Jellychin. She opened it, reading the words on it aloud, "*a good person*." The villagers mumbled to themselves about what all this could possibly mean when an arm made of letters shot out a hole in the cooking house and snatched another lurky turkey. And like before, bones, feathers, bits of meat and some rips of bread and spicy sauce shot out another window.

"Gobble yobble dobble!" Huhizs directed angrily at the village stewards, which translates as, "Ya'll need to reach back there and find your spines quick!"

They shook their heads completely befuddled.

But then the wind orphan Tessa came running up with another piece of the monster she claimed to have found a short ways off. It read, "*You're*".

That's when it dawned on Jellychin what might be happening and directly called Massey Massey, the lurky turkeys and the wind orphans around, giving them careful instructions. The group took Jellychin's initiative and gathered around the paella cuarto.

This is what followed: there would be a taunt by Massey Massey at one window, which syphoned a monster paper hand of letters, at which a wind orphan would rip away at specific letter groupings, causing words to fall to the ground. Jellychin would holler at another wall opening, prompting a lettered tentacle to lunge out, the lurky turkeys beak slicing like samurai.

The turkeys were making a pile of several more "*not*", some "*can't*", a few "*horrible*", a couple of "*hate*" and the children were making piles of "*pretty*", "*stupid*", "*stand you*", "*a real girl*". As this kept up, the fists and arms were looking more and more person-like. At about this point Jellychin motioned to Massey Massey to yank open the paella cuarto door. He did, which revealed the creature, which save the arms, looked something like a ghost made of streaming sentences.

The monster snatched one of the children that had gotten too close to the door for her peak at the screaming thing. It tried to put the child between two slices of bread but instead threw the girl out and into the sky, which out of nowhere was grabbed by a noche negra bird! It laid the wind orphan gently on the ground and looked at Jellychin.

"That was fortuitous!" Jellychin commended.

"Maybe" the bird shrugged. "I was flying around wondering what I was gonna do with the rest of my effin' life since I got kicked out of mounds for blasphemy, thanks to you."

"Really?"

"Really. I went from being known as BenTater the Breeze Maker to BenTater the Heretic to BenTater the Homeless in the span of about 3 effin' seconds."

The creature in the paella cuarto howled, seemingly warning that it was growing impatient and about to get jiggy with it, which brought Jellychin's attention away from the noche negra fowl, to the task at hand, and then back at the bird again.

"Since you're got time on your hands…" is how Jellychin's next favor of BenTater the Homeless was prefaced.

With an abandon that only a beast with nothing to live for could exude, the noche negra bird dove into the cooking house and into the heart of the spinning words and screaming. Each dive retrieved more paper words and at each escape, more and more of the miserable creature became unraveled.

Finally, all was undone, leaving only a small whimpering boy with gaunt eyes, weathered skin and plastic hair, grasping to a wooden toy. Roughly hewn, the toy really didn't look like anything specific but in certain slants of light, one could allow that might be a toy robot head with crayoned eyes drawn on it's face. Whatever it was, the child held the box up and made shooting noises with his split lipped mouth. Nothing happened but it didn't stop the scared child from repeating the action over and over.

Just about all the villagers there were moved with pity,

shaking heads and whispering prayers. Even the generally emotionless lurky turkeys and the noche negra bird cocked their respective feathered heads at the broken sight.

Yes, everyone felt all former rage give way to empathy for the pitiful little boy. Well, except one.

"Pathetic!" declared Compacist Grumps. "And terribly unoriginal! A poor excuse for a monster or a child either way. Defeated by slave turkeys, a rejected bird and unwanted children? Give me a break!"

Most everyone was so astounded at Compacist Grumps's gaul, they didn't notice the strands of words wrapping itself around the child again. But Jellychin did, she promptly pulled them off and with said materials gagged her former friend so she could say and hurt no more.

There was never any concrete direct connection made between Compacist Grumps and the destructive child, though theories abounded. The child was taken to the Salvage Shaolin monastery to be repaired physically and mentally, and was given to the specific care of a nun who was so full of love, it was said even the sun allowed her to hug itself. Eventually Grump Skid, as he came to be known, returned to the village with very little memory of all the trouble he'd caused and was absorbed into the skirt maker's ever expanding family.

As far as Compacist Grumps's fate, the best solution the

village stewards could come up with was to tie her up, put her in a giant basket full of fruit, nuts and candies, leave her at the front door of a more authoritarian city a good ways off, knock on the said city's door and run as fast as they could. This was not a very good idea as that after eating about halfway through the goodies, the authoritarian city managers noticed the awful woman in the basket. These sticky faced controllers promptly got into their dictator buggies and did a drive by of the village, dumping not only Compacist Grumps but their all empties from a taxpayer funded party the night before.

The stewards had to think of something else quick but were saved when a wandering blood mobile stopped by asking the village for donations. Ms. Grumps "donated" several gallons and was too dizzy to holler when the stewards glued her too the back of the mobile as it rolled away to the next town.

Not knowing what to do with a potentially dangerous robot, HumHead was left in his debilitating block of ice and stuck in the cellar of a village common building. But when a wandering legion of Puddle Sniffers attacked the village unaware the war was not only over but never with these particular people, the village — so proud of it's disorganization — couldn't locate the Sorrow Horn and found itself barely able to organize a village meeting to let every know how screwed they were.

So Jellychin thawed the robot head half way and straight up asked where was his allegiance, to which he answered, "To whoever owns me. That's how I was programmed. I'm as amoral and free of freewill as a dinner fork!"

So, along with face kicking wind orphans, eavesdropping turkeys, an injured but able D Dawg Tarps leading a unit of airborne self buttering popcorn kamikazes and a slew of other unique village warriors, HeadHum went into battle with his new lamp post body. The Puddle Sniffin' army retreated with their bruised heads buttered and aflame.

After that, HeadHum joined the lamp post force and particularly enjoyed patrolling and aiding on Grasstain street.

After nearly being wiped out by the legion, the villagers grumbled about their sucky decision makers. A new election was called for, at which Jellychin was nominated for the superior post. She did not want the job and so Massey Massey made up a ridiculous platform that vowed if his girlfriend was elected, she would ban the wintertime, give everyone a scoop of ice cream served in kitten skulls and that she would draw a smiley face on moon. I guess the people really hated the wintertime and kittens, cause Jellychin was elected "Head Village Steward In Charge". The beam sweeper didn't get kisses for a week, his girlfriend was so mad!

BenTater, having no peoples per se, became the Head Village Steward In Charge Judes' little buddy. The bird spied things coming from behind Jellychin and whispered some of her best speeches to her while on her shoulder (she had to remove the 'effins' before she repeated them to the peoples though.) And true to her word, Jellychin eventually made the noche negra bird a prophet amongst his own people. One day, the bird tribe having left a good play put on by some thespian bathrobe lizards, and in the mood for Lady-Be-Good-Bugs, decided to dine in Jellychin's back yard. It was quite the rude awaking when the bugs blew whistles and out of nowhere appeared cats with tiny saddles on their backs. The insects mounted the cats, reared back and, well, they had a big time with their would-be-eaters.

The decimated birds returned to their mounds and soon were writing poetry and fresh raps about how much better they would've been had they only listened to BenTater the FutureSeer.
So the exiled bird was asked back, and only agreed to return after he was promised a special hat and parade in his honor. He didn't have to ask for any girlie birds — they pretty much flocked to him without being asked.

All the heroes of this story went from being strangers and acquaintances to great friends and often got together in Rosemander's garden to sip acorn squeezins, trade stories and ideas while their host tickled her limestone piano. They eventually had many more troubles and the adventures that come with troubles, of which I hope to tell ya'll bout one day, providing I get the time.

One last thing, after they found a very perturbed woman glued to the back of their vehicle, the blood collectors put Compacist Grumps to work with their cause and that went okay for a while. But the mobile was attacked in desert transit by a giant vampsquito who not only drank all the blood that they had collected but drank all the blood in their own bodies. The entire crew dead, Compacist found that she was capable of officially recognized violence when the blood thirsty undead insect came for her and she in a unflinching act of instinct, impaled the creature with a blood bag stand.

That were not the end of her troubles because even though she had pledged allegiance to Brother Nature long ago, she really didn't know too much about nature itself. So finally at the point of starvation, she made a pile of burnable things, drained the blood mobile of it's fuel and made a fire. The fuel was a bit much and she lost some of her hair in the explosion. Nonetheless, she held the dead vampsquito over the fire and ate well for a few days.

The smell of cooked insect attracted the interest of wild desert children, who wore wooden planks for cloths and for some reason lived without adult supervision. They couldn't speak any kind of language but made motions that clearly indicated that they were asking for a place at her barbecue. Compacist obliged them and it found a feeling stirred she'd never felt before — one that comes from helping others who actually asked for it. After the children ate all she had to offer, they left patting the woman's hands and disappeared into the desert. Compacist almost chased after them to make them stay but stopped herself. It was a depressing next few days, she both missing that high of helping those with eyes not resisting her and also not knowing how to survive in the desert. She went out to sit on a large rock to die but while waiting for this to happen, she watched several creatures chase and acquire each other for food. Finally after many failed attempts, she accomplish the same, cookin' up some grand meals. And soon the wild desert children returned at the smell and again asked with their eyes, leaving when the food ran out.

And I can't report that there weren't many more internal trials for Compacist Grumps. But she never told anyone ever again — either through word or action — that they needed her help. And the broken world breathed easier because of it.

The Pains of K Shawty Bell

K Shawty Bell had been born on a dirt submarine because her dad was the captain and her mom worked in the sonar department. Actually that was all the crew they had on the craft. They met many rocks, roots, worms, moles and danged souls, but none of them K Shawty ever knew long enough to really ever call friends.

Then in her tweens, K's mom ran away (or dug away rather). The captain was heart broken and so set off to find the sonarologist of his dreams. But before he did, he surfaced the dirt sub outside a town named TJ and told K Shawty Bell to hang tight until he returned.

K Shawty Bell hung bout as tight as a young girl could and after a few days realized her parent's reunion might take a chunk of time. And so she began to place roots in the town, eventually becoming a productive citizen and making some real friends. But in spite of the latter fact, the complexities of friendship was still a very new thing to K and she enviably hit a few chuckholes on that particular road.

And on one otherwise pleasant particular day, Shawty Bell hit several friendship holes.

Cousin Pikelz — a famous hand clapper and finger snapper — was in TJ Town for a concert and K Shawty went, having a grand front row time! But when she was later telling her blind friend Bat Blindas about it, Bat sighed in a heavy way. "I would've loved to have attended. I wish you would've invited me."

K frowned at her own thoughtlessness and felt an ill stirring in her chest.

Later Shawty Bell was walking towards the woods and saw an old man standing still. The old man winced when K passed him, to which the girl asked if he was okay.

"You just stepped on my invisible hot steppin' kitten and broke his back legs!" the old man sadly reported. "Now it'll have to be in a wheelchair the rest of it's life and never be able to hot step again."

K never saw or heard the kitten but her chest got a little more queazy for the old man's sorrow all the same.

Finally K Shawty went on to meet her friend Bluhg LufDef to go rotten tree punching. At seeing her friend's protruding belly exclaimed, "Wowie, Bluhg! Either you're pregnant with twin elephants with bum thyroids or you just ate a whole honey suckle glazed fried butter baby!" (To clarify, they don't eat babies in K Bell's town but do have a delicious desert that's shaped and is the size of an 8 pound baby. It's a longer story to explain but chalk it up to an historical incident involving a particular terrorizing baby eating Uh Oh Monster with an honeysuckle allergy.) But yeah, Bluhg LufDef had in fact just eaten a whole honeysuckle glazed fried butter baby and not only felt sick from the gluttony but weren't none too proud of her belly pokin' out about now. So at K Shawty Bell's obvious observation, Bluhg burst out into tears and ran away.

At that point, K Shawty Bell could take no more of the horrible noxious feeling in her torso. And so the girl climbed up the Cliffs of Doug and threw herself off.

And as she lay broken in a dropped ragdoll stance, an old bone hair goat came along whom daily roamed the cliffs bottoms replacing any broken bones he came across with the bones growing in his hair. He did as much for K Shawty Bell and asked, "Why the swan dive of death, my dear?"

"I disappointed many people today and I don't know how to stop the terrible feeling that comes with it" the girl answered.

The bone goat nodded and offered, "Well, you might try and ask them for their forgiveness".

Well, as soon as her she got used to her new leg bones, K Shawty Bell ran off and did as much as the bone hair goat suggested. And everyone gladly forgave her and backed it up with hugs. (Even the invisible kitten reportedly purred for the girl, although K never heard it but became a believer when a blonde eyelashed jogger ran by and leapt over the spot where the crippled kitten was supposedly runnin' it's kitty motor!)

Life was pretty smooth for a spell for K Shawty Bell and in time she made some new friends and acquaintances in addition to the old ones. But of course in time she hit some friendship turbulence with those folks too.

At a Maker house pot luck, K found Alerbamer Faye's sarcastic tortilla casserole so delicious, she ate the whole thing in spite of the dish's never ending audible cynicism. Our girl felt that was the highest compliment for a cook but Ms Faye felt otherwise and left tightly grasping her empty dish with a little dark cloud over her head.

Then K and her friend Savannah da Pink Paper Heart Maka left the potluck and went on a drive in Sav's flyin' cubby pine derby car. At one point, K Shawty saw something interesting sticking out of Savannah's purse in the floor board and asked, "What's that?" while taking it upon herself to open the bag. Hundreds of pink paper hearts got sucked out of the purse by the high winds and made an aesthetically pleasing sky trail behind them, which made K laugh out loud in joy. But the same sight left Sav crying.

"It took me 10 years to make all those hearts and I'm only 12!" the da Pink Paper Heart Maka proclaimed in amongst gurgles of sniffs and tears.

So to get away from this day of disappointing people and

maybe get some cheering up, that night K Bell climbed up to visit Jen Jen the Banjo Fem's water tower home. They had a nice chatty time but at one point, K grabbed Jen Jen's banjo and not knowing how to play, pretended to know and sang badly all 23 verses of "*Our dawg's eatin' hunks of grass again*" and ended up breaking some strings around verse 18.

Jen Jen wrestled her instrument away from the girl before she got to conclude the song with an "Aaaaaaaamaaaaan" and asked K to go on home.

What I didn't mention about all the incidents on this day was that K Shawty Bell asked all the disappointed folks for their forgiveness. Everyone obliged her with their mouths but did not seem so warm as they had been before she disappointed them. It was if they were keeping a secret from the girl. And that feeling now gestating in her bowels invoked so much pain in K, she would do anything to make it end.

So K Shawty Bell went ice skating — in this height of summer. And so as she sunk into the bottom chill of the lake, she welcomed the water into her lungs. But a bubble bellied fish swam along up to the girl before her lungs were emptied of all the air. You see, the particular fish all day roamed the darkest waters breathing air back into sunk souls and after doing so for K, asked the girl "Why the heavy shoes?"

"I disappointed my friends and they forgave me but they're not acting as cool anymore."

The bubble gutted fish nodded. "Well, maybe if you try to both give them a little time to cool down and also try to undo what you've done, all might return to as it was."

So K Shawty Bell ditched the skates, swam back home and bought new sarcastic tortilla casserole ingredients, recovered some lost pink paper hearts and restrung a banjo just as the bubble gutted fish had suggested. And in time the girl's friends' warmth returned to as before.

But as you can guess, Ms Bell in time disappointed some folks on yet another day down the time trail.

Karney BarkyButt came to Shawty asking to borrow a week's wages to buy some expensive forehead jewelry. K hesitated because she knew Karney still hadn't paid Roberto the Record Baker back for some cash she borrowed to buy eyelash ornaments. With that in mind, Shawty asked Ms. BarkyButt what was the status of her debt to Roberto. Karney barked at K big time, accusing her of being the most greedy, petty friend ever and ran away! Shawty chased after her through the town pleading for Karney's forgiveness and waving the needed deniro. But BarkyButt cursed K Shawty Bell, her money and got away when K got slowed up by her own crying.

When she calmed down, K decided to go to the local hind leg barbecue pit — The Crooked As Is Delicious Pit — to eat a little lunch. Once there, a stranger asked to sit with her as they ate. She agreed and quickly the man got to talking about the politics of the town. He asked K Shawty what she thought of TJ's new mayor, to which Ms Bell pleasantly answered, "I don't agree with his fatalist policy on baby eating Uh Oh monsters, his stance on banana hair clips or really anything he advocates. But I hope he does the best for our town regardless of our disagreements."

At this the stranger started spitting up his hind leg batter and went into a tirade bout when anyone criticized the mayor's policies, it was just code for 'I hate the mayor's short pants.' (TJ had a history of short pants controversy, ranging from mean exposed knee jokes to outright violence involving mobs snatching shorts wearers and painting their bare legs the color of pants. These days it was just the easiest way to end any kind of actual intellectual dialogue when a short pants wearer was somehow in the mix.) The man ended his verbal barrage with the proclamation that K Shawty Bell was a short pants hate monger and that she'd wasted the hind leg he'd spit up.

K pleaded that she herself had short pants wearing friends who held her own views on banana clips and such, and tried to give him one of her un-ate hind legs. The stranger just marched off pointing his finger at the girl and chanted, "Hatin' on the short pants! Hatin' on the short pants!"

With other pit patrons staring with distaste at the girl and her appetite lost, K left her half eaten lunch to escape the bad scene.

From there, K climbed up and sat on terlerphone pole #38 to wait for her friend OrR, who told her to meet her there. But after an hour and no sign of OrR at their appointed time, Shawty climbed down and went home disappointed in more ways than one.

She later got an angry turtle shell phone call from OrR claiming she waited on top of Pole #27 all day long and she could never get that time back. K asked for forgiveness over the mix up and offered to give OrR a day of her life. (It has some religious origins but in that town they have a belief that people can give each other some of their life span. This author actually passed through there once and happened to save a fruit jar full of fuzzy worms on a flaming cucumber car. Many of the townspeople were so grateful, they gave me several months added on to my own life span. Now I'm not sure how long I had to live so I'll never really know, but the gesture is wonderful without a doubt). OrR refused to forgive K and spat at her day offer.

So utterly confused and devastated, K Shawty Bell car-jacked a hearse, raced towards the nearest graveyard, slammed into a creepy tree, which caused the little girl to go thru the windshield and a casket to pop out the back. Somehow the laws of physics were flaunted because both K and the coffin ended up into a freshly dug grave. Some gusty groaning winds blew the hole's dirt back in and over our friend and her new bed. And there K lay in a mess of glass, blood, hair, shredded dress fabric, ribboned flesh waiting to suffocate or bleed to death one.

After a little while K Bell heard some burrowing in the ground next to her casket and thought to herself, '*Daddy!*'. But it were just a cemetery mole which spends most of days liberating folks that had been buried prematurely. And at least in his opinion, the girls' burial was premature and so pulled her out of the ground.

After the two surfaced, the mole leaned K Bell against a headstone and applied spitmud he found in some corner of his mouth to stave the worser wounds. The grave mole then asked "Why the dramatic exit?" The girl retold her tale of her disappointing people, them not forgiving her or accepting her attempt at redemptive actions. And then of course the awful ill feeling that followed all these incidents, which were starting to eat at her innards.

The grave mole nodded wisely and after a a shake of the head said, "Well, little girl, some people in this world are just douche bags and there's nothing you can do about it."

K Shawty Bell was stunned that she actually wasn't entirely in the wrong this time. Although it would actually take her a few days to accept this fact fully, she smiled at the wise old mole and felt safe for the first time in a long time.

"So, Mr. Cemetery Mole, what do I do?" she posed trusting the creature completely.

The grave mole just shrugged and answered without thinking, "Try to start associating with people that truly appreciate you and aren't wound so tight."

K Shawty Bell nodded considering this. And then with an expectant look on her face asked, "Mr Grave Mole, will you be my adopted father?"

Never having been asked such a thing from anyone he ever dug up, the mole was struck. But he eventually answered with the first smile he'd allowed on his dirty face for some time. "Considering your epic concern for others, sure, I think I could stand you as a daughter!"

And off the two went to start their new family.

K Shawty Bell and the grave mole had many good endearing times — shopping at underground grub malls, spitting off of Jen Jen the Banjo Fem's water tower, searching the land for Savannah's still tumbling pink paper hearts, buying the Bone Goat some hair salad and the bubble bellied fish a nice shirt with the hem let out at the key bulgy places. They even formed a Cousin Pikelz tribute band that was apparently so good that it was said the hot steppin' cripple kitten wept at not being able to hot step to such blisterin' clappin' and snappin'!

Eventually the new family would begin to plan out a trip to try and find out what happened to K Bell's parents.

And sometimes in their new life together, they disappointed each other. But they also did much forgiving and undoing for each other as well.

www.ingramcontent.com/pod-product-compliance
Lightning Source LLC
Chambersburg PA
CBHW070335130626
46556CB00007B/2875